I0619761

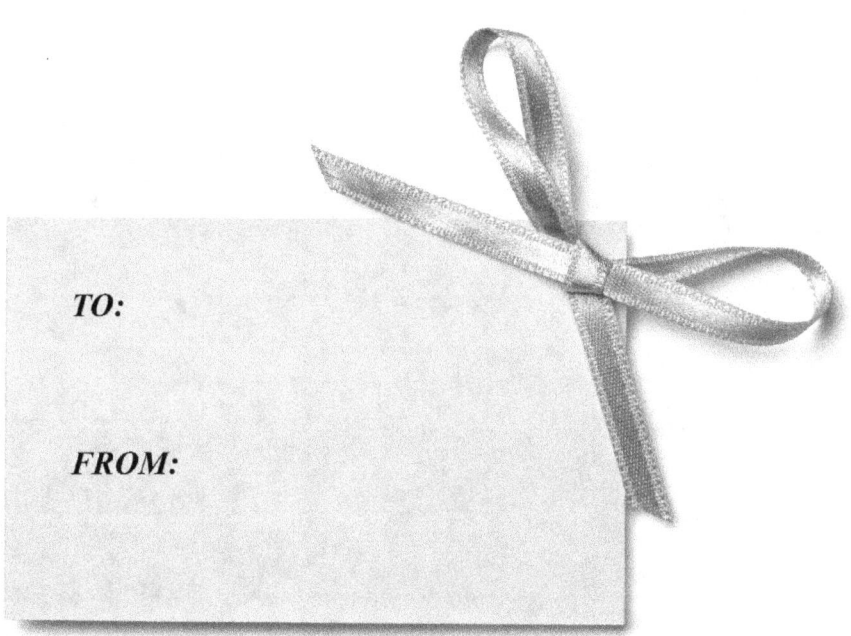

TO:

FROM:

The Vampire Who Saves Christmas

RICH BOTTLES JR.

Burning Bulb
PUBLISHING

The Vampire Who Saves Christmas
By **Rich Bottles Jr.**

Burning Bulb Publishing
P.O. Box 4721
Bridgeport, WV 26330-4721
United States of America
www.BurningBulbPublishing.com

PUBLISHER'S NOTE: This book is a work of fiction. Names, characters, places, and incidents are either the product of the author's imagination or are used fictitiously, and any resemblance to actual persons, living or dead, events, or locales is purely coincidental.

Copyright © 2017 Burning Bulb Publishing. All rights reserved.

Image credits (used under license from 123RF Stock Photo):
Santa Vintage Cover: Sparkstudio 14916589 ©: sparkstudio
Reindeer Girl for Epilogue: Kenny Kiernan 20685089 © kennykiernanillustration
Gift Tag Backcover: Karen Roach 5669631 © karenr
Script Girl: Lorelyn Medina 11378226 © lenm
1_Partridge: Lorelyn Medina 8360890 © lenm
2_TurtleDoves: Lorelyn Medina 8360872 © lenm
3_FrenchHens: Lorelyn Medina 8360893 © lenm
4_CallingBirds: Lorelyn Medina 8360854 © lenm
5_GoldenRings: Lorelyn Medina 8360828 © lenm
6_GeeseALaying: Lorelyn Media 8360889 © lenm
7_SwansASwimming: Lorelyn Media 8360915 © lenm
8_MaidsAMilking: Lorelyn Media 8360922 © lenm
9_LadiesDancing: Lorelyn Media 8360924 © lenm
10_LordsALeaping: Lorelyn Media 8360926 © lenm
11_PipersPiping: Lorelyn Media 8360929
12_DrummersDrumming: Lorelyn Media 8360927 © lenm
GiftTagforBottomofSignaturePage: picsfive 10599801 © picsfive

First Edition.
Paperback Edition ISBN: 978-1-948278-00-3
Printed in the United States of America

Dedication:

Dedicated to the memory of my younger brother Brian Bottles, whose death I learned about while writing page 59 of the script. Following the funeral services, I returned home to write the inflammatory lyrics for "Another Christmas Song."

CHAPTER 1

Twas not the night before Christmas, but some other night.

Twas a night in a quaint little Victorian era village, within one of those countries where it seems to be winter all the time.

The streets of the village were illuminated by whatever method people used back then, but one storefront in particular glistened and twinkled in a welcoming fashion that would attract even the most world-weary traveler.

Indeed, three such travelers stomped through the blizzard-swept streets that night, their bare feet sloshing into the snow drifts. Now before you start fretting over digital frost bite or stubbed-up toes on the hidden curbature, please understand that this wayward trio was not comprised of normal folk like you and me (or you at least), but were in fact demons.

The two female travelers were red-skinned and bare-assed naked, not like John-Smith-humping-Pocahontas Red Indian types, but the kind you might see in one of those Anonymous Bosch paintings. They were past their teen years, but their taut blossomed bodies indicated not by much. Their asses had a sheen and a smoothness like dual pairs of crystal balls, whose fortunes would be revealed to anyone brave enough to rub against them. And their titties! Oh god, their luscious titties seemed to burst forth from their sturdy chests like over-fertilized tomatoes, ready to be plucked by some vegan pervert. The girls' long braids of hair were red too, signifying that only the most daring of suitors should attempt to approach the sluts, because if one got too close to the bitches he'd quickly realize their eyes were also crimson.

But the male traveler was the weird one.

That burly black bastard had the hairy body of a wolf-like beast, although he walked on hooved back legs, almost like a human. He also had a human-like face, albeit an ugly human face, which seemed frozen in a displeased grimace amidst vacant ebony eyes. Goat horns jutted from the top of his skull, while his salivating mouth could barely contain a long sinister tongue. If allowed to unfurl, this mouth organ might reach down as far as his red-tipped canine cock, but let's not go there.

In one furry palm, he clutched the handle of a black riding crop, which he used to smack against the door of the aforementioned storefront. The girls licked their lips when the folded leather tip of the whip cracked against the wooden door, prompting them to remember how the very same implement had cut into their sensitive skin on more than one occasion.

After a few strokes, the door submissively creaked open, only to reveal a quivering half-sized human form, sporting some kind of green and brown suspendered lederhosen. "Ca-ca-can I help you?" greeted the wide-eyed midge.

"Y-y-yes, you can," mockingly growled the man-beast. "How about you scurry off and tell Jolly Ole Saint Nick that Krampus is here to see him on urgent business."

"Yes, sir, right away. Please come inside where it's warm."

The trio entered the store, which contained shelves full of handmade wood crafts that didn't interest them in the least. As the little man scampered out of sight, Krampus stood quietly with his arms crossed, impatiently tapping a hoof on the wooden floor. The only objects of interest to the girls were the flickering candles in the display window, which they quickly grabbed and took turns dripping hot wax onto each other's breasts.

They would hold the candles as steady as possible, allowing the molten wax to pool in the center of the candle sticks, and then they'd suddenly splash the contents onto the opposing boobs. Even the attention of the impatient Krampus was diverted to them, as they shrieked and giggled while the wax sizzled against their tortured skin and slowly coagulated. They excitedly breathed in the fumes of the vaporized wax as it passed through the stages of liquid, gas and solid matter, purring to the other not to miss their areolas and nipples. Soon their waxy breaths became more labored and they became light-headed in ecstasy, causing them to fall into each other's arms as the candlesticks tumbled harmlessly to the floor. Their sudden embrace was followed by passionate kissing, as they rubbed their wax-encrusted tits against each other, the body heat rewarming the wax once again.

"Um..."

"Lick the wax off me," one said as she broke off from the kiss.

"Um...

"Yes, chew the wax too, my love, chew it from my nipples."

"Um... excuse me."

Krampus and the girls begrudgingly turned to look down toward the squeaky voice in the center of the room.

"M-M-Mister Claus will see you now," the shocked elf stammered.

The girls seemed angered by the interruption, since not all the wax had been consumed from their breasts, but Krampus obliged them with his crop, smacking the candle remnants from their tits with a few strong but precise blows that almost buckled their already weakened knees. The little man waited patiently for the show to conclude, adjusting the crotch of his lederhosen as he lingered.

A brief stroll down the hallway brought the group to the door of Santa's office, which the small man obediently opened for the visitors. As soon as the guests were inside the gaudily-decorated and cluttered office space, the belittled butler closed the door and was on his way. Santa Claus, dressed in the red cloth and white fur as you'd expect, rose from his seat and extended his arms in a welcoming gesture.

"Ho, ho, ho! Come in and sit down! If it isn't my old nemesis, Krampus and his whores! Still thrashing and kidnapping the kids I've deemed to be bad? Ho, ho, ho!"

Both Santa and Krampus sat down, while the women flanked Krampus in the guest chair and began posing in provocative ways that only whores know how to do. Santa then pushed a plate of cookies toward his guests.

"Would anyone care for a cookie? They're fresh baked from Missus Claus."

The snatch snatched up some cookies, but Krampus refrained.

"Ladies, I don't believe we've been properly introduced," Santa observed. "But I bet you were once on the naughty list! Ho, ho, ho!"

Krampus begrudgingly responded, "Here is Succubus Two and Succubus One. These things here will bite you; they want to have fun."

"Eh, what?"

"Let's cut the small talk, Nicky. I've come here with a serious proposition for you."

"Do you mind if I enjoy a cookie while you brief me?"

"Yeah, actually I do mind, fat ass. Maybe you consume too many cookies, huh? Maybe Missus Claus is trying to kill you with all the sugary treats she provides. Did you ever think of that, tubby? Well, have you?"

"Now why would Missus Claus..."

Krampus leaned back in the chair and continued his pitch. "You're getting old, Santa. You're way overweight. I don't even know how you lift your proverbial bag of toys. I made all my rounds last Christmas, but my confidential source tells me you barely made it back before dawn from your little benevolent giveaway campaign. Also, I heard certain presents didn't get to the intended recipients, causing grief and disappointment to interfere on an otherwise joyous Christmas morn."

Santa's brows furled and he slammed a fist down on the desk, causing cookie crumbs to bounce into the stagnant air. "Now see here, Krampus, I don't know where you're getting your information, but need I remind you that nobody's perfect? Mistakes may be made, but you have to look at the big picture. You know, the greater good..."

"Spoken like a true Communist," interrupted Krampus. "You know as well as I do that you cannot continue at the pace you're currently on. You're getting more and more feeble while the greedy kids' wish lists are getting longer and longer... And you have what to help you?

One pint-sized punk, who doubles as a toy-maker and a butler? God forbid you ask Missus Claus to lend a hand, because she's too busy baking up another batch of your poison."

"Okay, okay, already," Santa submitted. "What exactly do you propose, Krampus?"

Krampus grinned and his tongue poked quickly from between his lips. He leaned forwarded and hissed, "Not only can I help you live forever, but I can provide an endless supply of pint-sized helpers."

"First of all, I don't know what a pint is. Second of all, you should know that Santa doesn't like liars."

"I don't give a flying fuck what you like, Santa, because I don't need to play nice to get any of your junky gifts," he spat. "But my proposal will help both of us. Succubus One and Succubus Two can provide you a magic elixir that will give you eternal life on Earth."

"But how does all this benefit you, Krampus?"

Krampus sighed, "I'm being overrun by the brats I kidnap every year. I barely have time to give each of them their daily thrashing. I weed out the older ones each year to try and make room for the newbies, but there's just too many bad kids popping up every Christmas. Personally, I blame the parents, but what can you do, right? The prospect of receiving lumps of coal from you never has worked, and the threat of being beaten by birch rods and whips by me isn't working either."

Santa added, "Perhaps if the children's socioeconomic situation improved, their behavior would improve also?"

"Oh, shut the fuck up with that bleeding heart bullshit! I say we combine our operations. I say we set up a warehouse in some remote place and we put my minion kiddies to work making toys for your so-called good kids. I'll be in charge of the manufacturing and you'll be in charge of the distribution. What do you say?"

Santa rose and extended his hand toward Krampus. "Ho, ho, ho! I say bring on the Succubi!"

***

After Krampus excused himself, Succubus One and Succubus Two found their way around the desk and approached Santa in his chair, causing the man to almost go cross-eyed when he attempted to ogle both girls at once. In stereo, both women leaned down and purred into Santa's ears, rubbing their fiery bosoms against his shoulders. Santa closed his weary eyes and rested his head against the back of the chair, a satisfied grin consuming his reddening face.

As the girls began licking either side of his neck, their hands reached down to Santa's crotch and began fidgeting with his oversized belt buckle. Not many folks know this, but Santa needed an oversized belt and buckle to hold in his oversized cock and balls, which the Succubi soon realized when the whole package burst forth as soon as the belt was unfastened.

As much as the women wanted to lower their ravenous mouths onto Santa's engorged genitals, they managed to stay focused on the job at hand and only provide a hand job, while their mouths searched for the sweet spot on Santa's throat. Santa soon felt the pang of desire when the fangs of the demons sank into his exposed flesh. But the pain of the bites was overcome by the pleasure of the female hands on his crotch, as one hand stroked his shaft and the other massaged his nuts. Santa's own hands did not remain idle as his fingers searched out the inner depths of the creamy crevices on either side of his chair.

Santa's ringing ears could hear both of the biters gulp down mouthfuls of his vital fluid, and he soon became light-headed as the blood being feverously pumped toward his brain was intercepted by the hungry blood-suckers. But Santa's blood still pumped freely down below, as evidenced by an increased stiffness that indicated Santa's special delivery would arrive sooner than later.

The accommodating hands suddenly loosened their grip on Santa's nether region, however, causing his own hands to end their expedition. With one final synchronized slurp on both sides, the women suddenly stood up and smiled down upon St. Nick, his blood still dripping from their quivering lips. They used their freed arms to wipe their mouths like messy babies, while Santa's free hands went directly to his abandoned dick.

The demons then leaned over the seated Santa and began passionately kissing each other, while the last remnants of spilled blood dropped onto the fat man's costumed chest. Santa then heard the rumbling of one bitch's belly, then the rumbling of the other tramp's tummy. Then one's body suddenly convulsed, leading to a similar reaction from the other. Both remained attached at the lips, however, while Santa slowed down his strokes to prevent a sudden eruption of his own.

Santa looked up at the tongue twisters just in time to see Succubus One pull away from Succubus Two and lower her head toward Santa's chest. The choking convulsions of Succubus Two prompted Succubus One to open wide her waiting mouth. A steady stream of sanguine sauce projected from Succubus Two and immediately overfilled the mouth of Succubus One, even though One tried her damnedest to swallow the hot steaming bloody load. Regurgitated blood splashed down onto Santa, but he maintained his steady strokes like a true unabated master of masturbation.

Violent convulsions then overtook Succubus One, who held her burgeoning belly like a pregnant mother trying to control the relentless kicking of impatient triplets. Her "morning sickness" quickly became a mourning sickness for Succubus Two, as the whores switched roles from catcher to pitcher (and Santa at bat, or course). A burst of bloody puke struck the open mouth of Succubus Two, almost knocking her out of bounds. Succubus One then waved her panicked hands to signal that a second wave was rising up her scorched esophagus.

But the upcoming upchuck wasn't meant for her cunty colleague. No! The girls' hands quickly reached into their sitting target's mouth, pried open his jolly jaws, and let loose a double-barreled blast into his crusty cookie hole. As soon as their oral ejaculate hit his uvula, his urethral ejaculate hit the ceiling.

***

Meanwhile, Krampus found his kink in the kitchen. Specifically, a middle-aged kink with a shapely body and few inhibitions.

As Mrs. Kink, err Claus, leaned over to pull a tray of hot cookies out of her old-timey oven, Krampus took the opportunity to smack her plump ass with his riding crop. Mrs. Claus yelped and jumped a bit, but did not drop the tray. She smiled when she saw Krampus in her kitchen and quickly placed the steaming bake tray on the counter.

"Oh, Krampy, don't sneak up on me like that when I have a tray in my hands!"

"But you always seem to have a tray in your hands," he responded. "Besides, you know I like the booty!"

Mrs. Claus and Krampus embraced and kissed like natural lovers, well as natural as a union can be between a demon hellbeast and a horny hellcat. Of course, there's really nothing natural about a French kiss where one lover's tongue is long enough to tickle the hiatal ring of the other's stomach.

Breaking to catch her breath, Mrs. Claus coughed, "So, did the old coot fall for it?"

"Like a pedophile priest falls for a choir, my dear."

Mrs. Claus stepped back slightly and began untying her apron, while Krampus busied himself with the unbuttoning of her blouse. She became slightly nervous when she saw his lascivious reaction to her revealed breasts.

"So, Santa told you about his days as a choir conductor for Priest Nicholas?" she giggled uncomfortably.

"Ha, ha! Good one, my dear! Now bend over the counter and press your tits into the hot cookie dough!"

"Whatever you say, Master."

Mrs. Claus reluctantly leaned her torso over the hot cookie tray, breathing in the pleasant aroma of hot cookies before she planted her tits across them. She struggled to keep position as the soft cookies enveloped her sensitive nipples in their gooey lava-like centers. The next thing she felt was Krampus lifting up her skirt to gain access to her own lava-like center.

He wasted no time burying his peculiar pecker into her slippery slit. Sweat soon began forming on her forehead and neck, pooling in her cleavage and dripping down on the sizzling pan.

Her face blazing red, she squealed, "Oh, please hurry, my nips are boiling."

"Perhaps I should've pre-heated your oven," he laughed while he continued to pound her pussy. "But you better stay still, unless you want my crop to punish those obstinate orbs."

"Yes, sir, I'll try..."

His dick slid in and out of her fuckhole with ease, and he considered moving up a notch to her tighter asshole, but was soon feeling that old familiar tingling in his balls. "It won't be long now bitch..."

"Thank you, sir," she gasped, almost at the point of passing out.

"Yes, and it also won't be long until we're together forever at a new, and very remote, location," he added, struggling to hold back his orgasm. "While you keep filling Santa's mouth with these cookies, I'll keep filling your holes with my icing."

Krampus suddenly pushed aside Mrs. Claus and shot his hefty load onto the cookie tray.

***

Outside Santa's shop, Krampus enjoyed a post-coital pipe smoke, appreciating the crisp coolness of the silent night. But his smoke break was suddenly interrupted when Santa Claus burst through the shop door. Santa now possessed a most menacing appearance and his uncontrolled rage was apparent to Krampus, who took another casual puff from his pipe.

"Krampus!" he yelled, stomping toward his new business partner. "What have your witches done to me?!"

Not impressed by the show of aggression, Krampus replied, "What's up, Father Christmas?"

Sans a proper collar, Santa grabbed Krampus by the scruff of the neck and got in the demon's face. With his virgin fangs glistening, Santa spat, "You said nothing about making me into a vampire, you loathsome bastard!"

"Would you have preferred a werewolf?"

Santa's eyes turned red with rage and he threw Krampus to the ground. "I'm not laughing, Krampus! You think this is funny?!"

Krampus slowly rose from the snow-covered sidewalk, looking momentarily for his lost pipe.

"Chill out, Nicky. There's only a few paths to immortality, at least here on Earth. Vampirism seemed to suit you best."

"How do you figure that?" he asked, still shaking.

"You work at night, right? Well, vampires can only go out at night, otherwise they'll shrivel up and die in the daylight."

"Shrivel up and die? What the fuck..."

"Well, spontaneously combust, however you want to say it. So, sorry there'll be no more afternoon strolls in the park for you. Not that you did a lot of that..."

"What about Missus Claus? What is she gonna say when she finds out she's married to a vampire?"

"Actually, Missus Claus was next on the appointment list of Succubus One and Succubus Two."

"What?!" he screamed as he started to run back toward the door.

Krampus grabbed Santa by the arm and said, "Hold on there, Santa. Missus Claus knows all about what's going down. And she knows all about the benefits of being a vampire."

"Benefits of being a vampire?"

"Yes, there are benefits of being a vampire, especially at Christmas. Follow me and I'll explain."

***

Unbeknownst to Santa, Succubus One and Succubus Two were already feeding from Mrs. Claus, in preparation of her transfusional transformation. But instead of taking the blood from the neck of Mrs. Claus, they positioned themselves on opposite sides of the Claus marital bed, and sank their bloody fangs into the brutalized breasts of

Mrs. Claus, taking extra time to lick the aching blisters on her nipples. The naked client in the center of the bed moaned as the Succubi continued to torture her already tormented tits. Each demon cupped its assigned feed bag with their hands, while Mrs. Claus used her hands to pleasure herself, feeling weaker and weaker with each passing gulp.

The bedroom seemed to spin for Mrs. Claus, ironically in the same direction her fingertips were encircling her swollen clit. When the dizziness became unbearable for her, she simply rubbed around her bud in the opposite direction. Aside from fingering her flushed flaps, Mrs. Claus realized she was losing control of her body and was defenseless against the famished fiends who flanked her.

"Oh god, oh god, my beautiful boobs are so sore... Will they ever heal? Please be easy with them..." she breathlessly called out to deaf ears.

Mrs. Claus had been asked to bring a large icing plunger/syringe from the kitchen and she soon realized the reason. When the Succubi began to dry heave and grab their contracting stomachs, Mrs. Claus watched as one placed the empty syringe against her mouth and began puking inside the long decorating tool. Then, like druggies passing a bong, the syringe was quickly handed to the other Succubus, who filled it to the rim with the stinking contents of her gut.

While one demon chick fitted the plunger into the syringe, the other instructed Mrs. Claus to "Turn over, honey."

If you've never had a large quantity of blood and puke squirted into your ass, it's hard to describe in words what Mrs. Claus was about to experience. But the scene was still titillating enough for Mrs. Claus to continue the fingering of her clit while the initial spurts entered her bunghole. The penetrating putridity caused the body of Mrs. Claus to spasm uncontrollably and she almost lost consciousness. She was experiencing tortuous teething pain before the last of the repulsive recipe emptied into her bulging rectum. An oddly-shaped gourd then sealed the deal and Mrs. Claus was left alone on the soiled bed to ferment, having not even achieved the orgasm she so desperately wanted.

***

In the meantime, an elf-like man named Alfie was in the fetal position on the floor of his closet, mumbling a prayer for protection.

CHAPTER 2

Krampus led Santa to a large Victorian mansion on the outskirts of town. You know, the kind of place that is eventually converted into a funeral home after a hundred years or so of more mortal use.

"... And we're here!" Krampus announced as he climbed the steps to the front porch.

"Here?" questioned Santa. "This is a whorehouse."

"Indeed it is, Santa. Indeed it is. Have you perchance visited before?"

"I usually don't deliver gifts to whorehouses," he admitted.

"Really? Well, what if the whores have children living amongst them? Are you going to just avoid such whorehouses?" Krampus asked.

"Yes, because those children would be the sons and daughters of whores, would they not?" Santa pointed out.

"I guess you've got me there, you judgmental prick," Krampus sneered as he tapped his crop on the front door. "Anyway, this particular place is not your everyday ordinary run-of-the-mill disease-ridden whorehouse. Oh no, no, no! This particular house of ill repute is owned by my good friend Rudolpho, and every whore inside was personally selected and supplied by me from my hoard of victims when they were still in their preteens. Rudolpho is going to assist us in our corporate merger and relocation plans."

The door opening coincided with the greeting, "Did I just hear my name mentioned?"

"Rudolpho, my friend!" answered Krampus, his friend.

Rudolpho can be stereotypically described as a tallish thinish individual of quite obvious African descent, who enjoyed wearing heavy fur coats with bright colorful trim, wide impractical hats, and garish gold chains, including his favorite necklace which featured a large diamond-studded letter "R" as the pendant.

"Gentlemen! Please come in. I've been expecting you!"

The three men entered the standard velvety-walled and dimly-lit bordello reception room. Rudolfo motioned for his guests to sit down in their choice of overly-cushioned chairs in the center of the room. "Can I offer either of you a refreshment?"

"Schnapps for me, thank you," Krampus spoke up.

Santa added, "I'll have an eggnog, if you've got it."

"But of course," Rudolpho responded before leaving the room.

Santa leaned toward Krampus and said, "You still haven't told me why we're patronizing a whorehouse."

"Well, if you must know, this is the place where you'll be able to pick up a quick meal - fast food, so to speak. Also, as I said, Rudolpho has offered to help us in our joint venture."

"And what's his incentive to help?"

"Not being killed by you or Missus Claus," Krampus answered. "You see, Rudolpho places significant value in his earthly existence."

On cue, Rudolpho re-entered the room and handed out the requested drinks.

"Thank you, Rudolpho," Krampus responded. "Now let's show Santa what's on the menu!"

Rudolpho picked up a small brass bell from a table and shook it. A parade of scantily-clad hussies soon entered the room and stood in front of the patrons.

Rudolpho, in his best lyrical voice, introduced the product, "You know Dasher and Dancer and Prancer and Vixen. Comet and Cupid and Donna and Blitzkrieg."

Rather than try to describe the feminine attributes of all eight ladies of the night, suffice it to say that there was a good mixture of ethnicity, hair styles and color, bust and butt sizes, height, etc. (but no fatties, of course). Dasher appeared jittery like she was tweaking, Dancer moved to a groove that was audible only to her, Prancer acted like she needed to use the bathroom, Vixen was licking her lips while studying the men, Comet and Cupid were twins, and Donna looked like your sister.

"Blitzkrieg?" questioned Santa upon hearing the name of the stumpy girl with the short-cropped black hair at the end of the line, who stared down at her bare feet and wore a loose black bodice that highlighted her pale white cleavage.

Rudolpho laughed, "Ah yes, Blitzkrieg is sort of our resident sullen Goth Girl. But who cares if a whore is happy, as long as she does what she's told, right?"

Krampus, waved his crop around, and added, "I'll thrash the attitude right out of her! Father Christmas needs happy concubines, dammit! Isn't that correct, Santa?"

In a show of support, Santa rose from his seat and approached the sad little woman. He circled her, checking out her sweet little ass, then leaned in from behind to whisper, "Who's your daddy?"

Before the girl could answer, if she even planned to answer, Santa grabbed her by the hair, and twisted her head down to reveal her anemic neck. He then savagely bit into her throat, holding her upright as he fed. A muted scream emitted from her terrified face, like she was caught in a silent horror film. The other women gasped aloud, but could not look away from the fiendish assault.

The Blitzkrieg attack aroused Krampus enough to call on his favorite whore. "Hey you, Dancer! Come over here and get on my lap, pronto!"

Without delay, Dancer executed a Grand Jete and a perfect Pirouette, which ended with a Split straight onto the waiting lap of Krampus. Facing the other women with her back toward Krampus, Dancer began grinding her taint on the exposed gland of Krampus. The hard hairy dick tickled Dancer with its static electricity, from her clit to her asshole, and made her face flush with unrestrained delight.

While being thusly serviced, Krampus leaned his head slightly to one side, so that he could see around Dancer's sweaty body and continue to keep a watchful eye on Santa Claus.

"Don't drain her out completely, Santa, you gluttonous pig!" yelled Krampus. "We need that sulking bitch for later!"

Santa allowed Blitzkrieg to fall to the floor. He wiped some excess blood from his beard with his red coat sleeve, and then stomped over to Krampus.

Rudolpho realized that the feast had finished and addressed the other women, clapping to get their attention. "The rest of you ladies, help Blitzkrieg back to the dressing room and prepare your costumes!"

Standing in front of the osculating doxy, Santa looked over Dancer's tossed hair and asked Krampus, "If I had drained the cunt, would she have become a vampire?"

"Nah, she just would've died," Krampus stated matter-of-factly. "You'd have to vomit the girl's blood back into her body to covert her."

Dancer's face began to show signs of distress, but Krampus didn't notice any interruption until he heard her start gagging and heaving.

"What's wrong up there, Dancer?" he demanded. "You don't like what you're hearing? Do we offend your delicate whorehouse sensibilities? Maybe Santa has something to plug your mouth with, so you don't throw up all over Rudolpho's fine carpetry."

"Yes," Santa agreed as he loosened his belt and dropped his pants. "Even I was careful not to spill any blood on the carpet."

Rudolpho laughed and added, "Indeed, Dancer, you'd best not regurgitate tonight's rations on this carpeting. Lord knows, not even Comet could get out such a stain!"

Soon Dancer had a good reason to gag, as Santa's engorged member invaded her mouth and throat. She held tightly onto the boney knee bones of Krampus as Santa face-fucked her and she continued to rub laps around the demon dong. A quick adjustment from Krampus allowed his provoked prick to enter her pasty pussy.

"Stay still and take it like a good little whore," Santa instructed. "Unless you want me to box your ears and pinch off your nose 'til you pass out."

"And that's nothing compared to what I'll do to you if you disobey," warned Krampus.

The desperate Dancer managed to breathe infrequently through her nose during the oral ordeal, but the scant oxygen proved insufficient to keep her conscious. Both gentlemen heard a deep groan from the girl the moment she passed out, and the suffering sound of the vanquished victim caused both of them to simultaneously blow their hot loads into her limp body.

Rudlopho applauded their synchronized performance. "Bravo, gentlemen! Bravo! It's not easy to wear out one of my whores!"

As Santa pulled up his pants, he nodded in acknowledgement to Rudolpho.

Rudolpho concluded, "I'll take care of this Tiny Dancer, if you'd kindly go to the backyard and wait for me there. I think I have something in store for you that you're going to like!"

***

When Santa and Krampus entered the backyard of the bordello, Krampus pointed toward the center of the snow-covered yard. "Check out what Rudolpho procured for you, using my specifications, of course!"

Santa walked up to the shiny object with a surprised smile on his face. "This is fucking awesome! You've really outdone yourselves - both you and Rudolpho! You must have known all along that I'd accept your business offer."

Santa had to take a step back to take in the full splendor of the bright red sleigh that stood before him in the yard, blinking his eyes to ensure that he wasn't dreaming. Inflamed torches were mounted on the front of the sleigh, causing the contraption to twinkle magically against the frozen earth. Two long leather harness lines were spread out in front of the sleigh.

"But what will we use to pull such a massive sleigh?" Santa asked.

At that point, Rudolpho barged from the backdoor, joyfully ringing his brass bell. Behind him trotted two lines of trollops costumed as so-called "pony girls." The girls wore leather strappings across their naked bodies, clip-on antlers atop their heads, and long-haired tails sprouting from their asses. Once the reindeer girls aligned themselves with the harnesses in front of the sleigh, the three men worked to secure them to the sleigh. Of course, Krampus had to smack a few of them with his crop to keep them in line.

"Go ahead and jump inside the sleigh, Santa," Krampus encouraged his partner once the girls were locked in place. "Take 'er for a spin around the village and see how she handles."

Santa didn't hesitate to climb aboard, grabbing a long bullwhip from the seat as he positioned himself in the driver's position. "Don't mind if I do, Krampus. Don't mind if I do!"

Santa cracked the whip against the bare back of the closest reindeer girl, who let out a piercing squeal and pushed against the girl in front of her. The sleigh jolted forward as Santa whipped the next closest girl.

Santa called out, "Now Dasher! Now Dancer! Now Prancer, and Vixen! On Comet! On Cupid! On, Donna and Blitzkrieg!"

***

Santa eventually drove his sleigh up to the front of his shop. Mrs. Claus must have heard the crying and pleading of the reindeer girls, because it didn't take long for her to emerge from their trendy place of business.

As she walked onto the roadway, she admitted, "That's quite an impressive rig you've got there, Mister Claus!"

Jumping off the sleigh, Santa agreed, "Indeed it is, wifey, and all courtesy of Krampus and Rudolpho!"

Mrs. Claus flashed her fangs and added, "I wouldn't mind sinking my new fangs into that pimp Rudolpho."

"Sorry to disappoint you, sweetheart, but Rudolpho is strictly off the menu for us. It's part of the agreement Krampus made with Rudolpho for his assistance. But you're welcome to dine upon any of these fine reindeer does here, although you may want to steer clear of Blitzkrieg, since she's been pretty-well drained by yours truly."

"Well, which one is Blitzkrieg?" she asked.

"If you look at their tails, all the tramps have their names tattooed above their asses."

"Fair enough," she responded. "I'll even provide my lucky reindeer with some cookies after I feed, which should restore her energy following the involuntary blood donation."

"Then you may want to give Blitzkrieg a couple cookies too, since she's still acting a bit sluggish."

"Oh, by the way," added Mrs. Claus. "Please drop inside the shop for a bit and see Alfie. He wants to speak to you about a private matter."

"All right," he agreed. "That little piece of shit never could handle change."

***

Alfie timidly followed Santa into his office and climbed onto the guest chair in front of Santa's desk.

"You wanted to talk to me, Alfie?"

"Yes, Santa," the lil' guy sighed. "There seems to be a lot of changes taking place around the shop and I'm concerned about what my future role will be."

"And what changes are you talking about?"

"Excuse me, Santa?"

"The changes you've observed," he clarified. "What changes are you talking about?"

"Well, for example, you and Missus Claus becoming blood-thirsty vampires, for one..."

"Oh, yes, there is that."

"And you conspiring with Mister Krampus, a known child-molesting demon from the depths of Hell."

"Changes indeed, my friend. You are quite observant, I must say."

"Uh, thank you, I guess."

"So, let me see if I've got this straight. You're worried that these miniscule adjustments to our business strategy may adversely affect your current state of employ?"

"Sorta, yeah."

"Alfie, my boy, how much are we paying you now for your butlering and wood-working services?"

"Nothing."

"Nothing, eh? As in zero?"

"Correct, sir. I get paid zero salary for my services."

"But we do provide you with room and board, do we not?"

"Yes, if you consider room and board to be sleeping in a closet and eating stale cookies."

"And now you're worried about losing all these benefits?"

"Well, I am a Christian and it looks like I may be the only truly good person currently involved in this devilish enterprise."

"Well, it's always good to have a decent person around to bounce ideas off of and keep us focused on our ultimate mission of altruistic philanthropy."

"I'm glad to hear that is still our mission, sir."

"Of course it is, Alfie! Just because I'm now a so-called blood-thirsty vampire and I'm teaming up with a demon from Hell, doesn't mean I don't want to provide all the good children with presents on Christmas Eve!"

"Okay..."

"Also, when we set up our new shop, some of your toy-making burden will be relieved and I'll make sure you get an actual room to live in, so your queer self can finally come out of the closet."

"My queer self, sir?"

"Excuse me, I forgot that your curtailed height causes a lot of things to go over your head."

"My curtailed height, sir?"

Santa sneered, "Is there anything else, Alfie?"

"Well, there is but I'm hesitant to say anything..."

Santa bared his fangs and yelled, "Out with it, fag! I don't have all day!"

Alfie stuttered, "I, I, I don't trust this Krampus fellow. I think he has a less than honorable interest in Missus Claus."

"Do you have any evidence of this serious accusation toward my new business partner?"

"N-n-no, sir, I just have my suspicions."

"Well, until you have proof, I'd advise you to keep your dirty-minded suspicions to yourself."

"Yes, sir."

CHAPTER 3

A vast wasteland of snow, glimmering in the moonlight, stretched out before a party of weary travelers. The only sounds in the night were the tramping of feet in the snow and the chanting of a marching tune. Succubus One and Succubus Two were carrying one of those litter-type carriage contraptions, like royalty used to be lugged around in before horses replaced the slaves. Krampus was snoring comfortably inside the carriage, well out of sight.

The marching refrain came from a chorus of female voices, pulling sluggishly on Santa's sleigh, their restrain interrupted occasionally by a yelp-producing whip crack. Joining Santa on the sleigh was Mrs. Claus and Alfie, who winced every time the leather whip cut into the tender flesh of the reindeer girls.

Marching, marching,
Driving through the snow,
Our hot bodies are freezing,
From our toesies to our nosies.
Marching, marching,
Hiking 'cross this ice,
Our battered legs are tiring,
While the whip takes another slice.
Marching, marching,
How long can we go on?
We're weak from their feeding,
And our souls are all but gone.
Marching, marching,
Oh look how we suffer,

Our hope it is fleeting
As our trek gets even tougher.
Marching, marching,
We're hungry and we're cold,
Our guts are all cramping,
From the plugs that we must hold.

From time to time, Alfie would raise a pair of opera glasses to his eyes, but usually could discern nothing in the distance. This time, however...

"De Place! De Place, boss! De Place!" the little man yelled up toward the big man.

Santa looked down on Alfie and snatched the opera glasses from his tiny hands.

A large castle-like structure could be seen emerging in the dark distance.

"He's right!" Santa announced to Mrs. Claus. "Our destination can be seen up ahead!"

He then directed his enthusiasm at the reindeer, via the whip of course. "Now, Dasher! Now, Dancer! Now, Prancer, and Vixen! On, Comet! On, Cupid! On, Donna and Blitzkrieg!"

Eventually, the travel party pulled up to a large stable house adjacent to the castle. Santa grabbed one of the torches from the sleigh and jumped down to the ground. Alfie followed him to the entrance of the stable and was soon handed the torch, along with a shovel that Santa found leaning against the wall.

"Alfie," Santa instructed, "see to it that the reindeer are locked into their stables and given some unfrozen water. Also, once you remove their tails, you may need the shovel to clean up."

"Yes, sir."

Santa motioned with his arm toward Mrs. Claus. "Come, Missus Claus, and let's inspect the facilities. Perhaps we can find some food for the reindeer. We want to keep them healthy and strong, after all."

"You got that right!" she replied, licking her chapped lips.

Santa, Mrs. Claus, Krampus and the Succubi approached the entryway to the castle. The huge wooden doors suddenly burst open, revealing Rudolpho in the threshold. He opened his arms wide in an inviting gesture and smiled at his friends, his gold teeth sparkling like brass knuckles during a mob negotiation.

"Ladies and gentlemen, welcome to Christmasland! The place where every good boy and girl wishes they could visit and hang out with Jolly Ole Saint Nick and his horny entourage!"

As the eager group walked past Rudolpho, he added, "No offense meant toward you, of course, Missus Claus."

"None taken, Rudolpho," the horndog replied.

Once everyone was inside and Rudolpho closed the massive doors, Krampus glanced around the warm parlor, taking note of the festive decorations, numerous wall torches and large fireplace. "I love what you've done with the place, Rudolpho!" Krampus gushed.

"Thank you, Krampus," thanked Rudolpho. "Let's do a quick tour of Christmasland, shall we? Follow me... We'll start with the bedrooms down this hall."

Rudolpho opened the first door they encountered in the long hallway. The spacious bedroom contained a large over-sized bed, a fireplace and other humble furnishings.

"This is the master bedroom, reserved for Mister and Missus Claus, of course," Rudolpho informed the onlookers - or inlookers, since they were crowded together looking into the room. "It features the largest bed I could locate in the fall catalog, considering Santa's massive accouterments."

Santa added, "Excuse me?"

"Also, please notice the absence of windows, which means none of that pesky sunshine can penetrate the room."

Mrs. Claus, who slyly winked at Krampus without Santa noticing, concluded, "Hopefully, there'll be some penetration in the room."

Santa added, "Excuse me?"

"Notice this empty side of the room, which is eventually where your new sleeping coffins will be placed. In the meantime, you'll have to sleep on the bed like us normal folk."

Santa added, "Excuse me?"

Mrs. Claus asked, "When will our sleeping coffins be ready, Rudolpho?"

"The construction will commence as soon as the first shipment of Krampus Kids arrives, which should be in a day or so, according to the traffickers."

"Yes," agreed Krampus. "Before the first brat even thinks about making a toy, I'll make sure they finish your permanent sleeping quarters... Then the bed can be used for... other activities."

Mrs. Claus smiled, knowing Krampus meant to fuck her repeatedly on the bed like the whore she was.

Like the ignorant cuckold he was, Santa insisted, "And make sure they use quality wood. I don't want to rest in some stinky pine box like a filthy peasant."

"We're well aware of your aversion to stinky boxes, Santa," Krampus responded.

Missus Claus added, "Excuse me?"

"I assure you, Santa," Krampus concluded. "It will not be long before both you and Missus Claus can finally rest in peace, so to speak."

Rudolpho motioned to close the door, mentioning, "Very well then, let's continue the tour."

Santa was the first to begin following Rudolpho, while Krampus allowed the Succubi to precede himself and Mrs. Claus. Krampus then whispered to Mrs. Claus, "Speaking of RIP, I plan to rip these clothes off you later."

"Promises, promises, Krampus," she answered. "First you'll have to find a way to distract the fat man long enough to rip off anything."

"Not a problem, sweetheart. Not a problem at all."

The characters approached the next door and waited for Rudolpho to open it. The red- and black-painted room with goat's head pentagram patterns across the walls interested the tourists enough to file inside past Rudolpho. There were three single beds in the bizarre room, plus a bunch of framed pictures adorned the weird-assed walls.

"I've taken the liberty of designating this bedroom to Krampus, and to Succubus One and Succubus Two. Notice the three beds, which can of course be pushed together as needed."

"Look girls," Krampus observed. "You won't have to sleep on the floor anymore."

Succubus One and Succubus Two jumped up and down and clapped wildly, as succubi are apt to do.

"Unless, of course, you disappoint me and I make you sleep on the floor," Krampus added.

"Krampus, have you noticed the pictures on the wall?" asked Rudolpho.

Krampus strolled over to a wall like a pretentious prick at an art gallery. Holding his hand to his chin, he nodded in appreciation of the images depicted in the pictures, which contained crude ancient Chinese illustrations of various graphic sex acts, like in that Carnal Sutra book.

"Ah yes, man's immorality to man, err woman," he pronounced. "Very nice. Very nice, indeed. Nothing like primitive porn to get the old juices flowing."

He then pointed to one picture and turned toward the others, stating, "Hey look, Missus Claus, this woman getting boned in the butt looks just like you!"

Santa added, "Excuse me?"

"Oh, Krampus," Mrs. Claus blushed. "You are such a kidder. Isn't he funny, Santa?"

"Yeah," Santa sneered. "Funny like a Shakespearean comedy, my dear."

After an uncomfortable silence, Rudolpho moved toward the door. "Let's continue on to my favorite room, shall we?"

Once again, Santa fell in behind Rudolpho and the Succubi followed next. Krampus and Mrs. Claus were the last to leave the room.

"Shakespearean comedy?" Krampus murmured to her shrewdly. "Of course, my favorite one is the Taming of the Shrew. Don't you agree, my little shrew?"

Rudolpho proudly led the group to his bedroom, which was immediately recognizable to Santa and Krampus as soon as the door was opened. Mrs. Claus may have recognized the decor too.

As the group entered the room, Rudolpho exclaimed, "Welcome to my less-than-humble abode! As you can see, I brought the furnishings directly from Rudolpho's House of Whores. I shall be staying on here at Christmasland as the head chef, whoremonger and general middle management associate!"

"As long as you let me bake the cookies," volunteered Mrs. Claus.

"But of course, Missus Claus," Rudolpho acknowledged with a quick bow.

"Yes, you're a regular Renaissance Man, Rudolpho," Krampus commented. "Perhaps that's what the 'R' represents on your gold chain."

"Why thank you, Krampus. I try my best."

Santa spoke up, asking, "Will there also be a bedroom available for my half-man servant, Alfie?"

"Actually," Rudolpho answered, "I'm sorry that I didn't think of designating a special room for..."

Krampus interrupted, "... for that little shit? Let him sleep in the closet for all I care!"

"Krampus! You hush!" scolded Mrs. Claus.

"Yes," added Santa. "I sort of promised the little fellow his own room here at Christmasland."

"Might I make a suggestion?" suggested Rudolpho. "Perhaps he can have a cot in the toy-making bunker where the children will be sleeping, when they're not working. I believe he'll be helping to manage that area anyway, am I correct, Krampus?"

Krampus grunted, "Humph, I suppose so."

Rudolpho concluded, "In fact, I planned on taking our group to the toy factory next."

When the group turned toward the door to exit, they all saw Alfie standing in the doorway with his tiny arms crossed.

"My ears were burning," he announced.

Krampus slashed the air in front of him with the crop, demanding, "Clear the way or I'll make more than your ears burn, you quarter-liter queer!"

The group, including Alfie, followed Rudolpho into the workshop area, which was equipped with various hand tools and supplies, such as wood and other building materials, along with work benches, etcetera, etcetera. There was also an assemblage of cots in one corner, and what appeared to be a staircase leading down to the basement in another corner.

Santa was impressed, and complimented, "Very nice, Rudolpho! I can see a great many toys being made in this workshop!"

"Thank you, Santa. I kind of bought out a hardware store and had it moved here."

"Yes," added Krampus, "and soon this room will be filled with the sights, smells and sounds of industry! The hammering and sawing of woodworking and metalcraft, and the cries and moans of the busy workers!"

Looking toward the mysterious corner, Mrs. Claus asked, "Rudolpho, where do those stairs lead in the back of the room?"

"Ah yes," he answered. "Those stairs lead to a special counseling room where Krampus will escort any workers who might fall behind on their productivity."

"Like a dungeon?" inquired Alfie.

Krampus pointed the crop in Alfie's direction. "I know, lil' man, why don't you scurry over to the sleeping area and pick out a cot for yourself before the workers arrive?"

Alfie glanced inquisitively at Santa, who nodded in response, and then Alfie stomped off to find a cot to nap.

Rudolpho clapped his hands to gain the group's attention and proposed, "Let's proceed! We still have a couple of special rooms to visit! Look! There's a special room right over there!"

Rudolpho walked the group toward a glass door within the workshop, which had a sign on it reading, "SANTA'S OFFICE." Rudolpho opened the door and allowed the curious to look inside the smallish office space, which contained a desk, bookshelf, and other typical furnishings.

"Ah ha," Santa proclaimed. "This is where I shall keep track of all the good children and read their wonderful Christmas correspondence!"

Krampus added, "And don't forget to keep that Naughty List up to date too, so I know who to pick up on my rounds."

"I haven't let you down yet, have I Krampus?" Santa answered. "You wouldn't know what to do if you didn't have access to my annual list of naughty children."

"Don't flatter yourself, fat man."

Santa added, "Excuse me?"

Rudolpho interceded, "Speaking of calories, we should all proceed to the room Missus Claus has been waiting to see! Yes, the kitchen!"

Alfie angrily rolled over in his uncomfortable cot as the group left the workshop.

The kitchen was an industrial-sized facility with a large coal and/or wood-burning stove, various pots and/or pans, a pump sink, and lots of spacious countertops and cabinetry. The group oohed and aahed at the state-of-the-art culinary gadgetry, state-of-the-art for that time period anyway.

"In here I just feel like a pampered chef," the self-designated chef Rudolpho espoused.

"Oh my," observed Mrs. Claus. "It's so humungous!"

"That's what she said," responded Krampus.

Santa glared at Krampus, and then walked toward a couple of large burlap bags piled on the floor. One bag was labeled as carrots and the other as potatoes.

"Rudolpho, are these bags for my reindeer?"

"Yes, sir, they are!"

"You think of everything, don't you?"

"Like I've said, I always try my best. I want to make Christmasland the best place ever!"

Santa picked up both bags and threw them over his broad shoulders like sacks of toys, then told the others, "While you all continue to explore the kitchen, I'm going to bring my girls some reindeer chow."

CHAPTER 4

While Santa was busy with the reindeer, feeding them and feeding from them, Krampus and Mrs. Claus became busy in his subterranean "counseling room."

Mrs. Claus hesitantly descended the stairs of the dark dank dirt-floored dungeon. "You requested my presence, Master?"

Krampus was in the center of the room, seated in some kind of early dental chair type appliance thingy. "I guess we need to set up some ground rules for when you meet me in the Counseling Room," answered Krampus. "Firstly, you should never address me down here while you are clothed."

Mrs. Klaus kicked off her shoes near the stairway and walked bare foot toward Krampus, unfastening her dress as she approached the demon.

"Just the dress at this time, bitch," he instructed. "I'll take care of the underthings."

By the time she reached the center of the room, Mrs. Claus stood in front of Krampus with her dress in hand, trembling in a white chemise that daintily covered her body from her satiny shoulders to her creamy calves. Krampus grinned as he jumped up from the chair. He retrieved her dress and draped it across the chair, protecting it from the dirt floor.

Krampus then took her sweaty hand and led her to a wall where a large wooden "X" structure loomed. The structure was at least six feet tall and was comprised of two heavy wood beams that crossed in the center. Four metal rings were attached at the outer ends of the beams. "Face the wall and spread your legs wide," he commanded.

Krampus leaned down and grabbed some nearby rope from the floor. He patiently tied a strand of rope onto each of her ankles and then secured the opposite ends to the lower rings. He repeated the process with her wrists and the upper rings, until she was spread out wide against the wooden "X." She couldn't help but whimper, even though she hoped he didn't hear her.

"Very nice," Krampus stated as he admired his work. "I hope the bindings are secure enough to keep you firmly in place, but still not cut off the circulation... Not that you could die, anyway, vamp whore."

Krampus walked to the opposite wall, where a variety of whips, straps and other implements of corporal punishment were displayed. He selected a long thin whip from the collection and immediately began swishing it through the air. Mrs. Claus knew he had returned and was standing behind her as soon as she felt the first slash cross her back. "Aargh," she extolled.

Her fists clenched, her toes curled and her major muscles tightened from the sudden pang of sharp pain.

"Soon both your body and your mind will know who is in control," he said as he wound up his arm for another full strike.

The follow-up strike crossed the first and solicited a similar response, along with the head of Mrs. Claus jerking backward. "Ugh."

Krampus continued working on her back until blood began soaking through the chemise and sticking to her scathed skin. "I-I-I fear I shall faint at any moment, Master."

"I do not permit you to pass out, you hear me?" Krampus demanded.

"Yes, M-master, you are in control..."

"Damn straight, I am," he added. "But to show you some mercy, I will now concentrate on your plump ass!"

Being a man, err demon, of his word, he cut the whip into her chemise-covered ass cheeks. "Yikes!" she yelled.

The thin chemise danced like a white flag under fire from an enraged enemy, accentuated by the battle cries of a defeated foe. "Ay yai yai, my fucking ass!" she cried as stroke after stroke tore up her chemise and her cheeks.

Soon her chemise was cut into bloody ribbons, her newly-revealed thigh muscles shuddering and convulsing after each subsequent stroke. She tried to twist away from the onslaught, but the ropes held her securely in place for each punishing blow.

"Now, let's go back up and shred the top of your gown!" he exclaimed in a fervor.

Mrs. Claus moaned, and soon slumped in her restraints, the ropes at her wrists being the only ballast keeping her battered body from buckling onto the floor. The upper part of her undergarment did indeed begin to shred, revealing blood-streaked welts that were most prevalent across her spine and her shoulder blades. Soon the tattered garment fell unrestrained to her feet, while her body remained attached to the wooden "X."

Now the tip of the whip curled freely around her side, biting into her tender breasts, but she could only whimper in response, having been brought to the point of near unconsciousness. She knew she did not have permission to pass out, so she fought to remain as responsive as possible. She braced her forehead against the wall and clenched her teeth while the whipping continued.

Krampus could hear her sobbing over the whip cracks and stopped his attack. He moved close to her, careful not to get any blood on himself, and quietly asked, "Do you think you've had enough?"

It took a moment for Mrs. Claus to stop crying and choking on her tears, but eventually she managed to murmur, "More. I need more. Please whip me like the whore that I am."

Krampus stepped back and responded, "Say no more. I'm happy to oblige. In fact, I grant you permission to pass out this time."

Which she quickly did.

Krampus dropped the scourge at her swoon, and his pretense, as he lustfully moved toward her. He grabbed her limp body at the hips and directed her bloody ass against his bulging crotch. Her subjugated sphincter proved no match for his sound sword.

Speaking of sounds, unconscious groans erupted from the throat of Mrs. Claus when Krampus began forcefully fucking her ass. Her guttural groaning was only surpassed when the throbbing of the cock caused its owner to groan like a gorilla at the sight of a Goodall. "Damn!" he screamed as his boiling hot juice shot into her massacred asshole.

He fell to his knees in exhaustion and stayed there until he mustered enough strength to cut Mrs. Claus free from the "X."

Now it was Mrs. Claus on the ground, as unresponsive as the day she first realized she had wasted her life on a fat fuck of a husband. Krampus leaned down and stroked her sweat-matted hair. Then he grabbed a clump of hair, lifted her head, and smacked the hell out of her face until she came to...

"Wha-wha..." the confused woman mumbled.

"Open your mouth, you dumb fuck, and keep it open!" snarled Krampus.

Although still not completely connected to reality, she did as she was told and soon had a mouthful of demon dick.

"Lick it clean, bitch," he told her. "Lick it clean or you'll be back on the rack."

Mrs. Claus gagged from the nasty appendage that had just wrecked her rectum, but licked and sucked on the semi-erect pecker until it was as clean as a Christmas chimney.

Meanwhile, an elfish peeper surreptitiously watched, and took notes, at the top of the Counseling Room steps.

CHAPTER 5

Standing impatiently like a pimp outside his best ho's motel room, Rudolpho waited on the icy platform of a desolate train station not far from the Christmasland castle. His arms were crossed to keep his thick fur coat as close to his body as possible to fend off the freezy breezes that swept across the barren winter landscape. Occasionally, he glanced inside the ticket window and sneered at the clerk, who was snuggly sleeping on a chair next to a furnace.

With still no train in sight, Rudolpho suddenly banged on the ticket window, almost causing the shocked clerk to fall on the floor.

The startled man angrily slid open the window and asked, "Can I help you?"

"Yes, can you tell me if the Polar Express is running on time?"

"The what?" asked the clerk. "What the hell are you talking about?"

Rudolpho pointed to the sign above the window, which read: PolEx.

"I assume Pol Ex is short for Polar Express?"

"No," snapped the clerk. "It's short for Poland Express, you pigmented Pollock."

Rudolpho reached inside his coat to retrieve his switchblade, but was distracted by a far off train whistle. "Never mind, smart ass."

The longer Rudolpho watched the train, the slower it seemed to approach. Even once it stopped alongside the station, it took a while for the conductor to appear. The conductor slowly climbed down to the platform, clutching a clipboard and being careful not to slip on the ice. He crept past a shivering Rudolpho and headed toward the ticket window.

The clerk slid the window back open.

"Hey, Bob."

"Hey, Bill."

"How's it goin', Bob."

"Same as always, Bill. How 'bout you?"

"Same as same as, Bob."

"How's the family, Bill?"

"They're fine, Bob. How's yours?"

"They're fine, Bill."

"How 'bout this weather, Bob?"

Rudolpho jumped in. "Excuse me, gentlemen, but it's damned cold out here and I'm waiting for an urgent delivery."

"Yep, this weather is really something, Bill."

"That's for sure, Bob. That's for sure."

Rudolpho seriously considered pulling his knife again, but the conductor raised the clipboard.

"Hey, Bill."

"Yeah, Bob."

"Says here I got a delivery for some fellow named Rude Dolphin, or something. You know him, Bill?"

"Can't say that I do, Bob. Can't say that I do."

Rudolpho, interjected, "Are you kidding me? I'm standing right, here. And my name is pronounced Rudolpho!"

"I believe that's the man you're lookin' for, right there, Bob."

"I believe you're right, Bill. I just need him to sign off for receipt of the delivery."

The conductor held the clipboard toward Rudolpho and then fished around for a writing implement in his multi-pocketed conductor's coat.

"Now where did that pencil go off to? I swear I had it not too long ago when I was doin' my doodlin'."

Rudolpho's left eye began to twitch.

"Maybe you left it on the train, Bob."

"Maybe I did, Bill. Maybe I did," agreed Bob. "'Cause I was just doodlin' with it not too long ago."

"Are you guys just fucking with me?" Rudolpho asked. "Or are y'all just retarded?"

"Patience is a virtue, my friend," answered the conductor. "Now if you'll just excuse me for a moment while I go back on the train to find my pencil..."

"What?!" exclaimed Rudolpho, immediately pointing toward the ticket window. "Bill here has a pencil in his motherfucking hand!"

"But that's a schedulin' pencil, not a doodlin' pencil," the conductor explained. "Isn't that right, Bill?"

"That's right, Bob," agreed Bill. "But maybe we can make an exception for Mister Rudedolphin, seein' he seems to be in an awful hurry and all."

"Well..." began the conductor.

"Well?" asked Rudolpho.

"Well?" asked the ticket clerk.

"Well... I guess just this once it'll be okay."

Rudolpho took the initiative to reach inside the window and snatch the pencil from the clerk's grip. "Where do I sign?"

"Right at the bottom will be just fine," the conductor answered. "If you can't write your name, you can just sign with your mark."

"What do you mean, if I can't write my name? You think I'm stupid or something?"

"Don't mean nothing by it, Mister Rudedolphin," the conductor replied as he watched the impatient man sign his name.

Rudolpho then tossed the pencil back through the ticket window. "Here you go, Bill. Be careful you don't doodle with that thing."

Ignoring the aggression, the conductor simply stated, "Follow me, sir."

The clerk mumbled, "Dumb Pollock."

The conductor led Rudolpho to a freight car, box-shaped, in fact. He pulled a large sliding door open with his clipboard-free hand, revealing a massive wooden crate inside the car. The crate displayed a red arrow on the side, pointing downward, along with the upside-down words: THIS SIDE UP. There was also a red-lettered warning: SEMI-FRAGILE.

The conductor pointed to a leather strap attached to the bottom of the crate. "I'm going to the other side to push, if you'll be kind enough to pull from this side."

"Whatever, Bob."

The conductor made sure to take the long way around the train to reach the opposite side of the freight car and slide the other door open. "All right, Mister Rudedolphin, I'm over here," yelled the conductor, once he was over there. "Are you ready to pull from your side?"

"Whatever, Bob."

As Rudolpho stood idly by, he heard the conductor announce: "Okay, then! Count-ah Three!...One!... Two!... Three! Pull, pull, pull, pull!"

Rudolpho didn't pull shit, but watched the crate inch forward a bit and halt. "Damn that's heavy!" whined the conductor, stopping to catch his breath. "I think we've almost got it, though! Let's go again! Ready? One!... Two!... Three! Pull!"

This time the crate moved all the way across the floor of the freight car and teetered on the threshold. "Stand clear, Mr. Rudedolphin! One more push ought to send it over the edge!" Rudolpho had already been standing clear.

Rudolpho watched as the wooden crate came tumbling out of the freight car and smashed apart in front of him, sending flailing bodies of screaming children across the ground like a Twister game interrupted by an earthquake. A dozen kids of all shapes, sizes, nationalities and emotional well-beings rolled around on the frozen ground, moaning and groaning like the spoiled brats they were.

The conductor looked down from the open freight car and exclaimed, "What the hell is that mess?"

"Santa's little helpers," explained Rudolpho.

"I was wonderin' what the air holes in the box was for," laughed the conductor.

"Well, now you know, Bob."

"Yep, now I know," concluded the conductor as he slammed the sliding door shut from inside.

Rudolpho waited a moment until the kids had settled down some, then clapped his hands. "All right, all right, already!" he called out. "Stop the dramatics! Nobody fucking gives a shit!"

The confused children slowly got to their feet, some picking splinters out of their exposed skin. Many were crying, while some were still in a daze, perhaps with concussions. They were all dressed in rags and covered in their own filth.

"Okay, I brought some strands of rope with me in the sleigh," announced Rudolpho. "While I fetch the rope, you urchins need to find you some broken slats of wood that you can tie to your feet. You won't make it to Christmasland without some kind of snowshoes! Your free ride is over, you hear me? You'll be hoofin' it the rest of the way!"

While the unruly urchins were strapping small pieces of wood onto their swollen feet, Rudolpho loaded the larger boards onto the sleigh. One piece of broken board resembled a paddle that his momma used to use on him when he wouldn't get up for school. Rudolpho used the board to get the reindeer pumped up for the journey back to Christmasland, beating each of their plugged-up asses until they were black and blue.

***

Once the new arrivals had arrived at Christmasland, Alfie wasted no time introducing himself to the fidgety fuckwads as they nervously sat at workbenches in the factory area, some rubbing their frost-bitten footsies.

"Santa will address you shortly... My name is Alfie, but you should refer to me as Sir. I am the shop foreman and I'll be supervising you in the making of toys that Santa will deliver to the good children on Christmas Eve.

"Basically, this process will work as follows: I receive the toy lists from Santa, which the good children have sent him. I review the lists and make notes as to what patterns or plans to use in the construction of the toys. Then I'll assign the lists to you workers, so you can begin work on the toys. It's important that you work on one list at a time, so no child's gifts get mixed up and we can avoid disappointments on Christmas morn."

Alfie walked over to some filing cabinets and continued his spiel. "This is where the plans for the toys are kept. If you have difficulty finding something or understanding a pattern, just let me know because I've built all these toys many times over.

"You all have some basic tools at your workbenches, but here against the wall are some others that may help you in the construction of certain toys. We also have plenty of paints, glues and other accessories. If you can't find something, don't hesitate to ask..."

***

Meanwhile, Rudolpho entered the kitchen while Mrs. Claus was baking another tray of cookies for Santa Claus.

"Excuse me, but Alfie is finishing up his orientation and the workers are expecting to hear from you, Santa."

Santa begrudgingly stood up from the table, responding, "Very well then."

"The cookies will be waiting for you when you return," sang Mrs. Claus as her husband stomped out of the room.

Rudolpho then turned to Mrs. Claus and announced, "And Krampus requires your immediate presence in his bedroom, Missus Claus."

"Very, very, well then!"

***

When Santa entered the toy shop, one child laborer was asking Alfie where the stairs led in the back of the room.

"Ah yes," Alfie responded. "Those stairs lead to a special Counseling Room where our product inspector, Mister Krampus, will

46

escort any worker who might be lacking in their productivity or their attitude. Believe me, you want to avoid such counseling if possible."

Santa made his presence known with a hearty, "You got that right, Alfie!"

"Well, hello, Santa! The workers have been waiting to hear from you!"

"Very well, then," answered Santa. "Would you kids like to hear a little song?"

The children cheered, expressing their enthusiasm for the jolly old coot's offer. As Santa sat on the edge of a table facing his audience, Alfie handed him a guitar. Santa strummed the strings to ensure it was in tune. "You're excused now, Alfie," Santa added.

"Yes, sir."

Santa played a few basic chords as an introduction, then sang for the children:

Because you're young, you may believe
That the very meaning of life
Is full of nothing but birds and bees
But there's also struggling and strife.
For I am here to tell you all
As your mentor and your friend
That some people's lives shall befall
To painful anguish that won't end.
Some people are born privileged
It's really not their choice
While others' lives are pillaged
And they'll never have a voice.

Life's not fair; get used to it
Your needs aren't worth my spit.
Life's not fair; get used to it
As your future turns to shit.

But even the doomed are useful
Yes even you workers can help
For you can serve the good people
As part of the proletariat.
So don't be jealous of others
Who have much more than you
Treat them like sisters and brothers
Who give you their chores to do.
Like Christmas is a time of giving
As Jesus's birth proclaimed
All your sins, He has forgiven
But your service is ordained.

Life's not fair; get used to it
Your needs aren't worth my spit.
Life's not fair; get used to it
As your future turns to shit...

CHAPTER 6

While Santa was busy bullshitting the worker bees, Krampus was all comfy in his red bathrobe, as he sat in a fluffy chair by his bed, reading from some nasty book and munching on something contained in a cup. He eventually heard a knock on the bedroom door.

"Come in, my dear!" he called out.

Mrs. Claus entered the room and closed the door.

As she approached Krampus, she asked, "What are you eating, Krampy? Are my cookies not good enough for snacking?"

Krampus glanced inside his cup and then held it out for Mrs. Claus to inspect. "I'm snacking on human teeth, sweetie. Would you like some?"

"Eww!" she answered.

"Don't knock it, hun. The consumption of human teeth by a demon provides a sexual virility that mere mortals can never attain."

Krampus placed his cup and book on a side table, then leaned back in the chair and opened his robe. "Check it out, Missus Claus!"

"I've got something for you to check out too," added Mrs. Claus as she unbuttoned her blouse.

Krampus jumped up, licking his lips in anticipation. "Did I fail to mention that eating human teeth also makes my tongue more versatile?"

Krampus proceeded to unbutton the rest of her blouse, flinging it to the floor, before pulling at the clasps of her dress and her undergarment. He stripped her nude while stroking his big dick with both hands. "Wow, that tongue of yours really is versatile!" exclaimed Mrs. Claus.

"And that's not all it can do!" promised Krampus, as his thong-like tongue poked between the legs of Mrs. Claus while she stood in front of him. The tip tickled her asshole, then slipped across her taint and finally separated her cunt lips, as it continued on its carnal journey up through her pube patch, over her tummy (stopping for a quick spin inside her navel), between her boobs and into her mouth.

Mrs. Claus initially gagged on the tip of his intruding tongue, a result of the ass sweat, pubic hair and belly button lint that it picked up along the way. She felt her knees go weak and immediately kneeled down in front of her master. As soon as Krampus withdrew his tongue from her mouth, the cavity was refilled with the throbbing girth of his organ grinder. His tongue found refuse elsewhere, exploring the smaller cavities of her waxy ears and her crusty nostrils. And when his tongue blocked her nose from inhaling, and she began to choke violently on his canine cock, his tongue quickly licked away her salty tears.

He accomplished all these frisky feats with his hands clasped behind his back, smiling down at his submissive concubine. Soon the left boob of Mrs. Claus turned the same beet red color as her face, as Krampus wrapped his tongue fully around the orb and tugged upward. There was still enough length to his tongue to allow for the nipple to be tweaked and twisted by the tip. Mrs. Claus managed to keep focused on the hard hot harpoon hammering into her throat, using her own tongue as best as she was able.

Krampus moved his body forward until Mrs. Claus fell backward onto the floor, leaving her mouth temporarily empty. Krampus climbed on top of her and slid his dick into her slit. His tongue then returned home to her mouth, twisting around her tongue like a giraffe claiming a fresh banana. As Krampus fucked her moist mound, he placed both his hands on her forehead, holding her head forcefully against the floor. He then began tugging at her entombed tongue, making her think he intended to rip it from her mouth.

Soon her bloodshot eyes balls bulged from their sockets, saliva sprayed from her gaping mouth and dark blood began to trickle from her flared nostrils. Even her ears ached as the blood racing to her head, along with the mounting pain, convinced her she was on the verge of a stroke.

But as frightened and panicked as she became, Mrs. Claus still managed to come - and come hard, even though her screams were muted by her tormented and twisted tongue. When Krampus shot his load into her quivering quim, he mercifully untangled his tongue from hers and laughed as she sobbed. She brought her fingers into her mouth to ensure that her tongue was still attached. The flood of tears from her eyes and the stream of blood from her nose made her choke as the facial fluids filled her swollen mouth.

Mrs. Claus slobbered and spit, "Owbah, yoush weally hwet meh!"

Krampus laughed even harder, mocking her temporary speech impediment. "Owbah, owbah, owbah, mah mowf be hweting! Owbah, owbah, owbah!"

"Thop ith, Kwamputh! Ith noth funnith."

"What?"

"Ah thed to thop ith!"

"Sorry sweetie, but I don't speak Retard," he chuckled, still positioned between her legs so she couldn't kick him.

Mrs. Claus then howled and cried louder.

"Oh, you're all right," teased Krampus as he rolled off her blubbering body. "I wouldn't risk detaching the thing that gives my cock so much pleasure."

Krampus managed to roll out of the field of vision, the field of vision as accessed through the keyhole of the bedroom door, the bedroom door where Alfie just happened to be stationed in the hallway. Alfie pulled his spying eye back from the keyhole, shook his head, and added a few scribbles to his notebook.

CHAPTER 7

Twelve-year-old 202499 jerked suddenly at his workbench when Krampus tossed a small wooden wagon toy in front of him.

"What the fuck is this, two-oh-two-four-nine-nine?"

"A s-small wooden wagon toy, sir?"

"Don't you mean a small wooden wagon toy with one wheel larger than the others?"

202499 tried pushing the small wooden wagon toy across the surface of his workbench and found to his dismay that it was indeed a small wooden wagon toy with one wheel larger than the others, as evidenced by its wobbly performance.

"It-it looks like the one wheel is larger than the others, sir," admitted 202499, who was now sweating profusely. "I will fix it right up and make sure it does not happen again, sir."

"Well, I think we need to discuss this in the Counseling Room, two-oh-two-four-nine-nine."

"The C-counseling Room, sir? I'm terribly sorry this happened, sir. Like I said, it won't happen again..."

"Come with me, two-oh-two-four-nine-nine," Krampus demanded, grabbing the boy by the shoulder. "By the way, the paint job on the wagon also looks like crap."

The other children at their workbenches pretended not to notice, but carefully watched out of the corners of their eyes as Krampus pushed 202499 toward the stairway at the back of the room. Sympathetic tears then formed in the corners of those eyes.

The demon's steely grip on his boney shoulder was painful enough to cause the boy to stumble slightly as he descended the steps and entered the dark subterranean room. The only object visible in the room was a bizarre-looking chair with a variety of restraints attached.

"Take a seat over there, two-oh-two-four-nine-nine," commanded Krampus as he gave the kid a quick kick in the ass.

As soon as the boy was seated, Succubus One and Succubus Two emerged from the shadows, wearing tight-fitting nursing scrubs, and began strapping the youngster into the chair. The panicked boy immediately started to struggle, but the Succubi had the sick situation well under control. "What - what's happening? Why are you doing this to me?" squalled 202499.

Once the Succubi backed away, Krampus explained, "Not only am I not happy with your work, two-oh-two-four-nine-nine, but I'm also not happy in my work. Some day I'd like to be a dentist. We need one up here. It's fascinating. You have no idea... Molars, bicuspids and incisors..."

"What are you talking about?" cried the boy. "You're scaring me!"

Krampus clapped his claws, prompting the reemergence of Succubus One and Succubus Two, one carrying a medical stand containing a collection of terrifying tools, like hand drills and tongs, and two taking position behind the chair.

"I'm just going to make sure all your teeth are uniform in size, so your mouth will work like a well-balanced wagon wheel," announced Krampus as he selected the plier-like tongs. "Open wide!"

202499 had no choice but to open wide, since Succubus Two had reached around the front of the chair and pinched his nostrils shut. As the boy took his first beleaguered breath through his patulous piehole, Krampus located a particularly awkward-sized wisdom tooth and grabbed hold of it with the tongs. Succubus Two had to place her other hand under the lad's chin in order to keep 202499's head steady while Krampus violently twisted and tugged at the tenacious tooth.

"Aiyeee!" screamed the boy as the nerve endings of his tooth protested its premature removal. His arms and legs strained against the restraints, then restrained again and again against the restraints with each new twist of the tongs. Clockwise, counterclockwise and pull; clockwise, counterclockwise and pull...

When the tooth finally let loose, blood spurted from the boy's yelping yap and Krampus almost fell backward. But he soon regained his balance and patiently dropped his unburied treasure into his favorite tooth cup. After regaining his composure, he told the boy, "I believe that was not your only wisdom tooth..."

***

Succubus One and Two carried 202499 to the Christmasland infirmary, under the direction of dental surgeon Krampus, who also instructed the demons to provide the boy with a "happy ending" to his ordeal. Unfortunately, 202499 did not immediately regain consciousness, so the Succubi simply licked the blood from the inside of his mouth and left him alone on a cot in the cold dark room.

In his dream state, 202499 was transported to the Island of Fucked-Up Toys. Rudolpho accompanied the boy on his dream journey, in hopes of finding a cure for syphilis. They traveled to the Island of Fucked-Up Toys on a blimp called Oh the Humanity, and soon discovered that an evil boy named Sid Phillips was attempting to destroy all the toys, who had become animated like in some kind of Bizarro novel. A Lesbian hippo named Clarice promised to help Rudolpho, only if the two visitors assisted her in tracking down the serial toy killer. 202499 tried to mend all the fucked-up toys, but Sid kept breaking them faster than he could fix them. Santa then arrived on the Island with his posse of reindeer girls and all the fucked-up toys came out of hiding to greet Father Christmas. With the all the toys gathered together, 202499 silently watched in horror as Santa joined Sid in setting fire to the fucked-up gathering. The burning toys shrieked in pain as dark smoke from their toxic paint rose in the polluted air. "No more toys! No more toys!" Santa yelled with glee over and over and over...

202499 rolled in his cot, spitting out more blood, as his feverish dream repeated itself over and over and over...

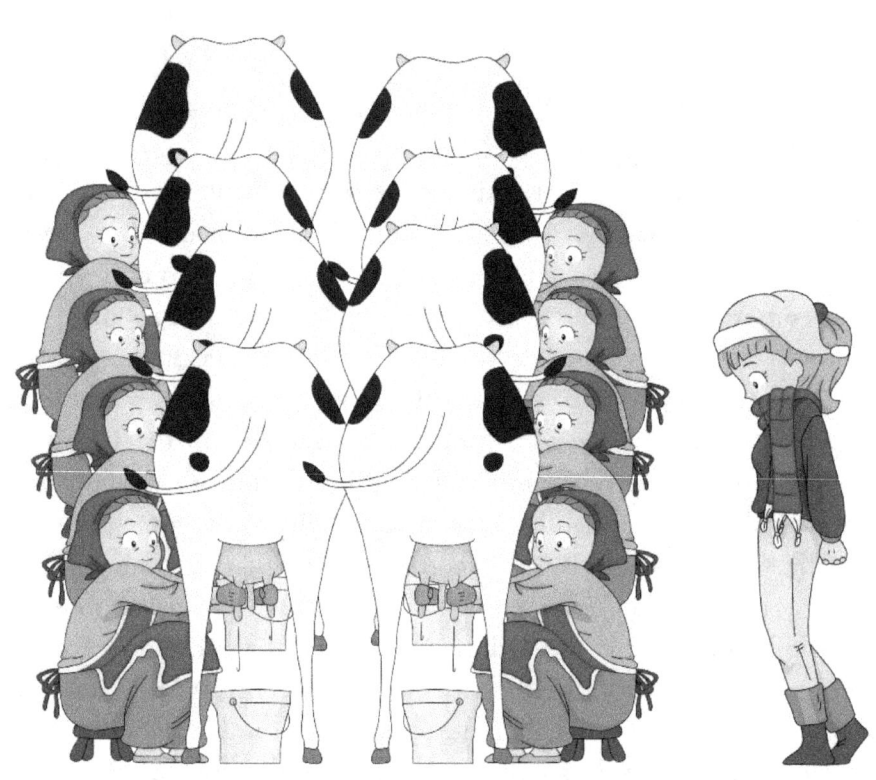

CHAPTER 8

As Christmas Eve approached, the number of children's letters to Santa increased and bags full of the pleading parcels arrived daily at Christmasland.

On one of those days, Santa heard a knock on his office door while he was working at his cluttered desk. Santa looked up from his work to see Rudolpho poking his head inside the office.

"Mail call!" Rudolpho called out.

"Just throw the bag down somewhere," Santa answered impatiently.

Entering the office with his pouty lip in full display, Rudolpho countered, "But I thought I'd help you go through it today. Pretty please, Mister Santa Claus... You promised that you'd let me help."

"Oh, all right then," begrudgingly agreed Santa. "Sit the fuck down."

"Thank you, thank you, thank you," Rudolpho excitedly replied as he sat down in a chair opposite Santa, still clutching the large mail bag to his heaving chest.

"Give it a break, Rudolpho, I'm in no mood for dramatics today," Santa cautioned. "Now dig out a letter."

Rudolpho placed the bag down on the floor in front of him. He then pulled out a letter with one hand and pulled out his switchblade knife with the other. In a matter of seconds, the blade snapped out of the handle and sliced through the envelope. The sheet of paper inside was then unfurled by Rudolpho and held up to his near-sighted eyes.

"Ah-hem," he cleared his throat. "Dear Santa..."

Rudolpho then stopped to chuckle and waved the paper in front of Santa.

"Oh, look!" Rudolpho laughed. "The little retard spelled Dear as D - E - E - R! Isn't that precious?"

"Just read the damn thing, Rudolpho!" Santa yelled.

"Okay, okay, already," Rudolpho acquiesced, before clearing his throat again. "Ah-hem... Dear Santa, my name is Mary and I've been very good all year. Please bring me a pony and the appropriate riding tackle. Some straw would also be nice. Thank you kindly, Mary."

Santa stood up, reached over the desk and swiped the letter from Rudolpho's hands. "Give me that! She'll get a doll and like it!"

As Santa wrote nasty notes on the paper, Rudolpho busied himself opening another envelope from the mail bag.

"This next one is from Billy," Rudolpho announced. "Ah-hem... Dear Santa, this has been a very hard autumn and winter for me and my family. My father has become ill and can no longer find work. My brothers and sisters don't want any toys for Christmas, but if you could bring us some food and maybe some medicine for father, it would be greatly appreciated. God bless you, Billy."

Rudolpho lowered the letter and solemnly looked at Santa. Santa grimly looked back at Rudolpho. Both men's eyelids began to twitch. Rudolpho then tumbled off the chair as both men burst out laughing. RROFL!

Sitting up on his knees with his hands clasped in front of Santa, Rudolpho cried out, "Oh, oh, Santa, my name is Billy and I don't want any toys for Christmas. But perhaps Missus Claus could cook us up a nice pot o' stew for delivery? Light on the salt and onions, please... Ha, ha, ha!"

"Ah yes," Santa guffawed. "And maybe I can bring some hot chicken soup for papa!"

***

While Santa was busy talking mishmash with Rudolpho, Mrs. Claus and Krampus were in the Christmasland kitchen mixing up their own amalgamation.

"Cook me up some Chicken Soup for the Soulless," urged Krampus, wrapping his arms around Mrs. Claus from behind.

"But what if Santa interrupts?" she coyly asked, realizing that Krampus was tugging at her apron as she stood before the large island-like counter in the center of the kitchen.

"Don't worry," he whispered in her ear. "Rudolpho is keeping the fatman busy in the office."

The devilish grin of Mrs. Claus was sensed by Krampus, even though he stood behind her, and was accented by her verbal consent. "In that case, let's get cooking," she purred.

Krampus immediately tore her clothes off and tossed her naked body onto the kitchen counter. Krampus then tore through the cupboards - all except one, to the relief of Alfie who was hiding inside.

Krampus pulled an assortment of canisters out of the cabinetry and the icebox, lining them up beside Mrs. Claus on the counter. He also grabbed a wooden mixing spoon and a large funnel from the collection of cooking instruments on the wall.

"But before we proceed with our recipe, we must preheat the oven!" he announced as he began using a paring knife to peel off the bark-like exterior of a large phallus-shaped ginger root.

"What do you plan to do with that?!" exclaimed Mrs. Claus.

"Heat up the coals under the oven, dear," Krampus explained as he shoved the shaved root into her southern-most stove pipe.

It didn't take long for the juices of the raw ginger to begin burning the mucous membrane of her raucous rectum. Mrs. Claus instinctively reached down to remove the painful plant from her posterior, but Krampus slapped her naughty hand away. "It burns, Krampus! Please take it out!" she begged as she rolled around on the cool counter.

"Oh, quit acting like a colicky baby," Krampus chastened. "It's not like I rammed a garlic bulb up your butt. Now that would really burn your vamp ass!"

Krampus grabbed the funnel and jammed the narrow end into her warming cuntoven. "Ow! Be careful with that thing," she protested.

Krampus carefully poured flour into the funnel.

He used the handle end of the wooden spoon to force the powdery ingredient through the funnel into her snatch. He followed the flour up with some caster sugar and a few cups of milk via the funnel. Then came a clump of butter and a couple whole eggs, which Krampus simply pushed into her snatch, thanks to the lubricating properties of the butter. Next was a dash of salt, which was administered via a thick long salt shaker.

"Okay, so the recipe doesn't call for yeast, but it looks like that final ingredient already comes with the bake pan," Krampus joked, as he jumped up onto the counter and positioned himself atop Mrs. Claus. "Now to mix it all up with my dick!"

"Doh!" she squalled.

"No cake!" he corrected.

The clingy combination of components felt cool around his cock. But the hodgepodge heated up once his thrusts became more hurried and harder. Liquids and solids squished from around her assaulted snatch, including stuff that may or may not have been inserted by Krampus. "Oh please, Krampy," cried Mrs. Claus. "It feels like my crotch is about to explode!"

"That's not all that's about to explode!" warned Krampus as his body tensed up to add the icing to the cake.

The Claus woman's belly shook like much more than just a bowl full of jelly, as her orgasm met with his in a carnal collision, the likes of which has never been equaled within the best French restaurants nor the worst Paris bordellos.

When Krampus rolled off his culinary conquest, he whispered, "I haven't forgotten it's your birthday. Let me get you some cake."

Mrs. Claus was too exhausted to protest, even when she felt the wooden spoon enter her womb. As Krampus scraped around inside her with the spoon, he reminded her that he was also an expert abortionist if she were to ever need his services in that regard.

"Now open wide," she finally heard him say. "Happy birthday!"

The strange brew assaulted her taste buds and made her gag as she tried to swallow her birthday present. She vomited the moment Krampus pulled the sloppy spoon from her manhandled mouth. The broken egg shells and other debris scraped raw her palate as she projectile puked a putrid pile toward the chef. He jumped back to dodge the regurgitation and laughed, "Well, I guess my concoction is an acquired taste."

Mrs. Claus spun her convulsing body around on the counter until Krampus was positioned between her legs. "Then eat up," she sputtered.

Alfie could smell the sickening aroma from inside his cupboard and he committed its racy recipe to memory.

CHAPTER 9

Okay, so now it's Christmas Eve...

Santa was again sitting behind his desk in the office when he acknowledged a knock on the door, but this time the knocker was Alfie.

"Enn-ter!" Santa answered dramatically in his best stage voice.

Alfie sheepishly entered the office, carrying his clipboard, and shut the door.

"I've completed the pre-trip preparation review and all seems in order for tonight, Santa," announced Alfie. "Your so-called list has been checked twice. The designated presents are wrapped and loaded on the sleigh, except for some last minute requests that are still being worked by the toymakers. The reindeer have been fed, beaten and their tails embedded."

"Fine," grunted Santa. "If there's nothing else, you can leave... I'm a busy man. It's Christmas Eve, you know."

Santa looked back down at some paperwork on the desk, but Alfie was hesitant about leaving.

When he didn't hear the shuffle of little elf feet, Santa glanced back up and noticed Alfie still standing in front of his desk.

"I said, if there's nothing else, then ski-daddle!" he reiterated to the idiot.

Alfie stuttered, "W-well, Santa, actually there is something else, though I'm, ahh, hesitant to..."

"Out with it, elf!" Santa yelled.

"Okay, okay," whined Alfie. "Do you remember back at the old shop when I expressed concern over the trustworthiness of your business associate Mister Krampus?"

Santa squinted at Alfie and stretched out a wary acknowledgement, "Yyyyyyessssss?"

"And you said not to bother you with my suspicions unless I had proof?"

"Yyyyyyessssss?"

"Well, I believe I've got proof."

"Proof of what, Alfie?"

"Proof that Mister Krampus has been having an affair with... with... with Missus Claus."

Santa laughed and replied, "Are you joking, Alfie? I sincerely doubt Missus Claus would let that demon dick bone her."

Alfie timidly approached his employer with the clipboard and held it out, in trembling hands, for Santa to view.

"Here are my n-notes of what I've witnessed..."

Alfie began flipping through page after page of stickman figure type drawings, which vaguely illustrated some kind of undefined activity between the stick figures. Santa developed a perplexed look on his face, like he couldn't comprehend why he was being shown a bunch of ignorant and indistinguishable child-like drawings.

When the page-flipping ceased, Santa patiently inquired, "Alfie, what the fuck are you trying to show me?"

"Well, these are my notes of the liaisons I've witnessed between Mister Krampus and Missus Claus."

"So, you expect me to believe they let you watch them fuck and take notes?" Santa inquired a little less patiently.

"No, no, no," Alfie answered. "I hid and watched. They had no idea I was around."

Santa sighed and said, "Listen, Alfie. You may be a good Elf on the Shelf kind of spy, but you suck big time at drawing. I have no idea what these pictures are supposed to be. At first, I thought you wanted me to play Hangman or something."

"Oh..."

"But I have an idea," Santa continued. "Why don't you just tell me what you saw?"

Alfie glanced around the small cluttered office like he was looking for something or somewhere to stand. "Oh-kay, I'll try..."

Alfie put down his clipboard on Santa's desk and moved a couple chairs to make a wider space on the floor. Alfie then leaped into the open space like a spotlight had suddenly been lighted at the spot.

"Okay, okay, okay, so I sneak down the dungeon steps [mime creeping movements], and low and behold, [surprised look] there's Missus Claus tied face-first to this like large wooden cross [spread his arms and legs like he's crucified], she's wiggling around like she's trying to break free [grind movements], but like she's not really seriously trying to break free, because her wrists are tied to the top part and her ankles are tied to the bottom part, well, okay, it's more like a big wooden X than a cross, so her legs are spread, but she still has her underpants on like white lacey briefs and a top, but Krampus is standing right behind her with a whip and he starts slashing at her back and her ass [violently swinging arm], and she starts screaming like she's panicking, trying to get her wrists free, but she can't, of course, and Krampus just keeps whipping away [more arm swings] and her underwear starts ripping and falling apart and her skin starts getting these red slash marks that are turning black and blue, but Krampus doesn't let up and Missus Claus just keeps squalling, although soon it just sounds like crying and then sort of like a low whimpering, then Krampus suddenly stops and checks on her, I guess to see if she's fainted or something, but I guess she's awake 'cause I hear her whisper [in a female voice], 'More - I need more, please whip me like the whore that I am,' and Krampus is like [heavy male voice] 'Say no more, I'm happy to oblige,' and would you believe, he starts whipping her again, but not for too long, 'cause I think she really does faint after a while, which is when Krampus drops his whip and his pants and jumps in behind Missus Claus, whose body is hanging limply from the cross or X or whatever you call it, he directs his giant cock straight up Missus

Claus's asshole [more grinding], I swear, no lube or nuthin' at all, and I kind of hear her groan like involuntarily, which gets louder and louder and louder as Krampus keeps pounding and pounding and pounding away at that tight ass, until Krampus is the one groaning as he shoots his load right up her poop chute, but he doesn't stop there, oh no, he's still not satisfied with his disgusting conquest, 'cause he cuts her down from the cross and starts slapping her face [slapping the air] while she's on the floor, until she sort of regains like semi-consciousness, at least enough for Krampus to force her to lick his filthy cock clean, and she laps it up like she's having a dream about visiting an ice cream store or something [licking invisible cone]... Then there's another time where both of them are in Krampus's room, and I'm like outside looking through the keyhole, and I see Krampus teasing Missus Claus with his long nasty beet red tongue [wagging tongue], which he's sticking in her mouth, in her ears, in her nose, in her cunt, in her ass, in her arm pits, licking everything from her eye balls to her taint, leaving no crevice untouched, while Missus Claus is squirming and panting, begging for more licks and pokes, as his tongue literally wraps around a tit while the tip tweaks her nipples like a baby calf suckling the mama milk cow, then I see them collapse on the floor in a heap and Krampus gets on top of her and they kiss like only the French can kiss, but he doesn't stop there, 'cause I could see his tongue just twirl around hers and start tugging it, like he's trying to tear her mouth organ right out of her flushed face, while at the same time, he's driving his hard cock into her wet fuckhole, her body is like convulsing, but you could tell she's loving every second of it, until finally she comes, but still can't say anything 'cause Krampus has her tongue tied up with hers, so she can only spit and drool in response to the huge orgasm she's having, which causes Krampus to come while Missus Claus is sputtering 'Owbah, yoush weally hwet meh' and that's a direct quote... Then there was the time they were in the kitchen together and Missus Claus was on the counter and Krampus was pumping sugar and spice all into her girl parts like she was some kinda of decadent cake or fancy pastry or something, and she's like, 'Eat me,' and he's like, 'You know what they call this recipe where I come from?' She says, 'No, what do they call this type of recipe where you come from?' Well, he starts licking and slurping the sweaty sweets from her snatch, until he looks up and answers, 'The Aristocrats!'

Santa jumped up and shouted, "Shut up! Shut up, damn you! I get the point! You saw them fucking! Christ, I'll deal with this shit later!"

CHAPTER 10

Somewhere in a typical Victorian home, a mouse laid dead. Stockings were hung. Children were snug. You get it...

In the master bedroom, the lady of the house was sound asleep and wearing one of those babushka-kerchief thingies on her head, like she was one of those Muslim types. Hubby was also wearing head-cover, specifically a night cap, probably to keep his delicate ears from freezing in the drafty abode. Although his ears were covered, the man was still able to hear the festive sound of sleigh bells outside in the yard and you can bet your ass he jumped out of bed to see what was the matter.

He tore open the shutters and lifted up the window, only to be astonished at the sight of Santa Claus standing behind a humungous sleigh --- a sleigh with a bunch of mostly naked women attached to it. And when Santa began cutting into the back of one of the women with his bullwhip, causing the shrieking victim's blood to spray across the snow, the curious man at the window passed out from the sheer shock of it all.

Once the husband began to "come to," he thought there might be an intruder in the bedroom.

And then, in a twinkling, the husband heard in the room, the slurping and gnashing of a man in costume... As the husband shook his head and continued to "come around," down on his wife St. Nicholas came with a bound... The neck of the wife, Santa held tight in his teeth, and his mouth encircled her throat like a wreath... Santa had a scary face and a big round stomach, which shook when he fed, like some beast in a panic... Santa was vile and vicious, a right evil old elf, and the husband gasped as he watched Santa, in spite of himself... A glare from Santa's eye and a twist of the head, soon led the husband

71

to know he soon could be dead... Santa whispered some words, as he continued his work... Then Santa fed more from the wife, until he turned toward the jerk... Pointing his finger at the husband's sniveling nose, Santa gave a quick nod and out the door he did close.

The man sat frozen in fear until he heard Santa's voice bellow from outside: "Happy Christmas to all, and to all a good night!"

***

Later that night in another home, a pair of preteen fraternal twins were sort of sleeping in their candlelit bedroom. The sister broke the silence in the room by softly whispering to her brother, "Brother, are you awake?"

The brother's bed was next to the sister's bed, but the brother did not respond to the soft whisper.

"Brother, are you awake?" she asked in a not-so-soft whisper.

"W-what?" mumbled the brother.

"Are you awake?"

"I am now," he confirmed. "I was just dreaming of dancing sugar plums."

"Well, dear brother, I fear that I cannot sleep for it is Christmas Eve."

"Which is all the more reason for you to try to sleep," he responded. "Because Santa may not visit if we are awake."

"Poppycock," she disagreed. "We've been good all year, so I doubt Santa would skip our house just because I have a bout of sleeplessness."

"Good night, sister."

After a brief pause, she added, "Brother, I have an idea."

The brother tried to ignore her, but she reiterated, "I say, brother, I've got an idea."

"What, sister?" he resigned. "What idea do you feel the need to tell me about in the middle of this solemn night?"

"I say we sneak down to the drawing room and we hide ourselves somewhere."

"Why ever would we want to do that?"

"So we can see Santa arrive, of course, you numb skull."

"Calling names will not help me agree with your silly idea."

The sister then rolled out of her bed and sat on the corner of her brother's bed. "Oh, I'm so sorry, brother dear," she begged. "Please come downstairs with me. I promise we won't get caught."

The brother sat up in bed. "How can you promise that?" he asked.

The sister grabbed her brother's arm and replied, "Because I just know we won't be caught, that's how."

"Okay, okay," the brother agreed. "But if I don't get a new spinning top for Christmas, I shall be quite displeased with you."

The twins tip-toed out of the bedroom and crept down the stairs to the drawing room. Moonlight reflecting off the snow outside made visible a loveseat-styled settee against one wall and a fireplace against another wall. Of course, two matching stockings were hung by the chimney.

"Come," she whispered, holding her brother's hand. "Let us hide behind the settee."

As soon as they were hidden behind the furniture, sleigh bells were heard outside.

"Oh joy, sleigh bells, brother. Do you hear them? Santa must be outside."

"Hush girl, or someone will hear us," he cautioned.

A tense silence then covered the residence, until a loud squeaking noise of a door handle was heard in the adjoining room.

The sister sighed, "I think Santa is trying to get in through the front door."

The brother whispered back, "Is it locked? Do you think Santa is unable to obtain entry?"

"Let us approach the hallway and ascertain whether or not the door is locked," she suggested.

The two tip-toed through the entryway of the drawing room and peered down the darkened hall toward the front door. The knob was twisting violently and the entire door was shaking on its hinges.

"Look brother," she observed. "The door indeed appears to be locked."

"So that means Santa cannot enter?" he asked.

Suddenly the twisting of the knob ceased and a loud pounding sound erupted, like someone was attempting to kick in the door.

"That doesn't sound good," the girl cried. "I'm scared."

"I think we need to go back to our hiding place," he said.

The children began walking backward, backing into the drawing room and keeping their eyes focused on the frightening hallway. Thus, they didn't see the pair of heavy boots dangling down from the chimney. Santa and his bullwhip burst from the fireplace just as the kids began to turn around.

"What are you brats doing up at this hour?!" Santa demanded, cracking the whip toward them.

The brats screamed and ran into the hallway.

"Get back here, right now, you two!" he yelled before starting his boot pursuit.

When Santa reached the hall, the children were no longer in sight, but that didn't stop him from looking into every room along the way, until he came upon the bathroom. Inside the bathroom was a bathtub with a curtain surrounding it. Santa rolled his eyes at the conspicuousness of the hiding place.

As Santa approached the curtained tub, he exclaimed, "Ah ha! I know where you are, so you'd better come out!"

The terror-stricken twins erupted from the curtain call like eager understudies seeking a standing ovation. Santa nary had time to react. He missed his grip on the girl's shoulder, but managed to grab hold of the boy's neck with his left hand. Santa then used his right hand to unfurl his bullwhip toward the girl, successfully getting the leather to wrap around the child's slim torso.

As the captured girl squirmed to remove herself from the whip, Santa asked the boy, "Are you the good little boy who wanted the top?"

"Yes!" he cried.

"Then check this out!" Santa laughed as he violently jerked back on the whip, causing the girl to spin around like a berserk ballerina.

Eventually the dizzy damsel collapsed on the bathroom floor in a ball of confusion, causing Santa to laugh all the harder.

He then looked down at the bewildered boy and snarled, "Unless you want to see your sister really get whipped, you'd better tell me where your mother is!"

"M-my m-mother, why?"

Santa tossed the boy against the wall and demanded, "Dammit, boy, where is your mother's bedroom?!"

As Santa approached the cowering carcass, the boy blurted out, "She's upstairs, the second door on the left... P-please don't hurt her."

"I'm Santa Claus and I'll do as I please!"

Santa exited the bathroom, leaving the crying children behind, and headed for the drawing room and the stairway to horror. When he reached the master bedroom, he observed the boudoir to be aberrantly bare. Thus he rolled his eyes again at the conspicuousness of it all.

He stomped over to the large bed, leaned down, and tossed the heavy furniture into the air. The horrified housewife was thusly revealed underneath and was promptly pounced upon by Santa. After a few moments of feeding, he whispered something into her obedient ear.

A gasp emanated from behind him, causing Santa to turn his blood-encrusted face toward the children trembling in the entryway.

"Mama!" shrieked the sister.

"Where's papa? What did you do with papa?" boldly asked the boy.

Santa jumped to his feet and yelled, "I thought I told you two to get to bed?!"

When Santa left the property on his sleigh, papa was still banging on the front door trying to get back into the house.

***

Even later that night in yet another home, two single-sized beds occupied the master bedroom. One bed contained a snoring father, oblivious to the world around him, and the other contained a praying mother, wary of the world surrounding her.

The mother prayed as she lay(ed), "And dear God, please keep our family safe from the evil that permeates this world. In Jesus's name, I pray. Amen."

The door to the room creaked open, but nothing was visible in the hall.

The mother climbed out of bed and walked cautiously to the open door. Before closing it, she looked into the hall to make sure that all was quiet.

She mumbled to herself, "That is strange, for I am certain I sufficiently secured that door in the closed position."

Once she was back in her bed, she prayed, "Dear God, strange things happen frequently in this house and no explanation can be discerned. If evil lurks in our holy home, please protect us from whatever haunts these premises. In Jesus's name, I pray. Amen."

The door to the room creaked open again.

"Oh my," she called out. "Is someone there? Is that you children, still awake on this Christmas Eve?"

Her husband snored in response.

The wife climbed back out of bed, murmuring, "That faulty door brings such a draft to this room, I must have my husband fix it tomorrow. Perhaps with that new tool kit I acquired for him as a present."

The woman shut the door again, this time wiggling the knob to ensure that the latch bolt was latched into the bolt hole. But she soon heard the door open again from behind as she returned to her bed. She immediately dropped to her knees in front of the bed and clasped her hands atop the blanket. She soon felt someone's breath breathing down the back of her nape.

Low and menacing, Santa spoke, "I heard your prayers, mother."

She gasped when she heard the wicked words. Praying louder, she begged, "Dear God, please, please, please protect me from..."

Santa grabbed her hair and pulled the woman to her feet. "Don't you know who I am?" he asked.

"N-no," she cried, holding her eyes tightly shut. "Are you here to hurt me?"

"Only if you scream."

She opened her eyes to gaze upon the strange man. "Who are you?"

"Are you dense, woman?" he asked. "Look at my stupid red costume... This is Christmas Eve..."

"Are you Saint Nicholas?"

He let go of her hair. "Bingo. We have a winner."

"But why are you in my bedroom?"

"Because I need your help downstairs."

"Must I? Can you not just leave me be?"

"Listen, do you want your children to get their gifts or not?"

"Well, I suppose, but cannot my husband assist you downstairs?"

Her husband snored at the appropriate time.

"Just be a good wife and let the man rest," Santa advised.

"All right I guess..."

The woman followed Santa down the stairs to the great room, as opposed to the drawing room of the previous narrative. Santa's bag of gifts was on the floor in the center of the room, while the walls were covered with numerous crosses and crucifixes of various sizes.

"What can I assist you with?" she asked at the bottom of the steps. "Were you perhaps expecting cookies and milk? For I fear we forgot to set them out this year."

Santa thoughtfully answered, "Well, that would've been nice, but that's not why I brought you down here."

"Oh," she responded. "Then what do you need?"

Santa pointed to the walls and explained, "I can't set out any presents in this room until you take down every single cross from these walls. Just the sight of them makes me queasy."

The woman's eyes widened in wonderment. "You want me to remove my Savior's crosses from the room? Are you not aware of the true reason we celebrate Christmas?"

"Bitch, I don't give a shit why you celebrate Christmas, but if you want me to leave presents for your brats, you best get your butt moving on the revamp."

"But..."

"And if you continue to piss me off, I'll rip your fucking throat out!"

The worried woman hurriedly began collecting the religious trinkets, mumbling something about walking through the valley of the shadow of death. She didn't stop until the walls were bare and her arms were full. "Where should I put them?" she asked.

"You, my lady, may shove them up your ass as far as I'm concerned! Just get the damned things out of this room!"

"Yes, sir," she obeyed, taking her collection to the hallway and placing them on the floor.

"Now come back here and get on your knees in front of me," he commanded.

The woman begrudgingly obliged.

He instructed, "Start praying to me, like you were doing upstairs."

She began crying and asked, "Pray to you?"

Santa reached down and grabbed her hands, forcing them together.

"Yes, heathen," he impatiently answered. "Entwine your fingers and pray to me as your Lord and Savior."

"But you're not my..."

"Did the God you were praying to protect you from me?"

"What?"

"I know you're not deaf," he sternly said. "I asked you whether this Entity you've been praying to was able to protect you tonight from the likes of me."

"Perhaps my faith just isn't strong enough when..."

"Bullshit," he exclaimed, flashing his fangs. "If you want me to protect you from a certain death tonight, then you'd better start prayin' to me and you sure as hell better mean it!"

The mortified mother prayed, "Dear Santa, I pray for your protection. I do not want to die tonight..."

Santa smiled, kneeled down beside her, and warmly said, "Very good, my dear. Now pull down the collar on your nightgown and show me your neck. It's time for your baptism."

He bit into her jugular and fed, finishing with a whispered blessing.

***

Similar scenarios played out in domiciles across Santa's route on that hallowed night, each visit ending with Santa whispering sweet somethings into the docile ears of the domestic homemakers.

CHAPTER 11

As dawn began to break on another glorious Christmas morn, everyone inside the Christmasland castle were sound asleep, having been driven to exhaustion in their preparations for Christmas Eve. Then the sounds of screams from multiple mouths awakened the cast and crew.

A child laborer was the first to hear the screams and she immediately woke up Alfie. "What is that horrible sound, sir? Who is screaming? It sounds like lots of people outside are in trouble. Please wake up, sir!"

Alfie sat up and listened to the frightening sounds. "What the hell is that?" he mumbled, shaking his head to fully wake up.

Alfie rolled out of his cot in his elfy PJs as the rest of the workers began crying out in fear. "Hush now!" he instructed. "I'm going to investigate! You all stay put and try to keep calm, for God's sake!"

The screams emanating from outside the castle continued as Alfie removed a torch from the wall and lit it in the fireplace. He then hurried out of the workshop and scampered down the hallway, just as the other adult residents were emerging from their bedrooms with torches of their own.

Mrs. Claus asked, "Does anyone know where that screaming is coming from?"

"It sounds like it's coming from outside the castle," answered Rudolpho.

"Follow me!" ordered Krampus.

The screams ceased as the group exited the castle and headed toward the stables.

Looking ahead, Mrs. Claus gasped, "Oh my god."

"Holy fucking shit!" added Rudolpho.

Just ahead of the stunned group was a large bloody pile of naked female bodies, some of them still morbidly twitching in death throes. The fractured female faces, which could barely be discerned through the blood and gore, displayed the full terror and torment that they had just mercilessly endured. The bare arms and legs were twisted and tangled like the limbs of a fallen tree. All their throats were slit open and still oozing their cruory contents.

Backlit by the dawn, Santa suddenly appeared triumphantly at the top of the heap. Like a conqueror standing victorious above a vanquished battlefield, he stood stoically with his fists lodged firmly into his sides and his elbows jutting out. His eyes appeared red as lasers as he bared his fangs and looked directly at Krampus and Mrs. Claus.

Santa's booming voice caused snow to avalanche down from the roofs of the stables and the castle: "You two are fornicators!"

Alfie, who was cowering behind Rudolpho, retreated back inside the castle, unwilling to witness the carnage any further.

Santa descended from the dune of the deceased and stomped toward Mrs. Claus and Krampus. Mrs. Claus collapsed to her hands and knees in the snow and began bawling hysterically.

"Santa, Santa, Santa," Krampus droned. "If you had read the fine print of our contract, you would've clearly understood that..."

"Shut the fuck up, Krampus!" spewed Santa. "I don't give a shit what the contract says, our business relationship is over!"

As Santa looked down in disgust at his sniveling spouse, Krampus suggested, "Let's not be hasty, Santa, we can always get new reindeer. Isn't that right, Rudolpho?"

Still in a state of shock at the sickening scene unfolding before him, Rudolpho mumbled, "What-Whatever Santa wants..."

"There ya go, Saint Nick," urged Krampus. "You heard the man. Whatever Santa wants, Santa will get. So let's you and I work this thing out like responsible business partners."

Santa turned to Krampus and replied, "There's nothing to work out! I'm hereby retired from this bullshit!"

"But you can't retire..."

"The hell I can't!" he shouted. "When I had the children's mothers under my spell tonight, I commanded them to provide gifts for their brats on Christmas from this point forward. Let the parents take care of their own damn kids!"

Krampus countered, "But how in the hell am I gonna know where the bad kids are if you don't keep track..."

"Krampus, are you not paying attention?! We are through, capiche? We're done! Caput! Take your Succubus One and Succubus Two and Suck-Up Rudolpho, and leave Christmasland, ASAP!"

"Whatever tubby," Krampus angrily retorted. "But I'll have you know, I've been pursuing other business prospects outside of here and I planned on leaving anyway."

"Good for you, motherfucker! Now get out of my sight and let me deal with my cheating wife!"

***

Once Alfie was back inside the castle, he raced to the workshop, where he found the children still in their cots, with blankets covering their heads. They were all trembling and whining, filled with dread over whatever terrible event had been occurring at the castle.

"Listen up!" Alfie announced. "Your work here is done and you need to leave Christmasland now! You're all in very grave danger! Santa has gone berserk and no one is safe! Follow me and I'll show you where the coats and wooden snowshoes are that I made y'all for Christmas... Don't ask me where you can go. You just have to go. Now!"

***

Back outside, Santa kicked Mrs. Claus over onto her back and straddled her shaking frame.

"How could you do this to me with that demonic piece of shit?!" he demanded.

"Please forgive me, Santa!"

"Give me one good reason why I shouldn't tear you apart, limb from limb!"

"Please, honey, it was all Krampus! He put me in a trance and I was forced to do whatever he commanded... Just like you did with those mothers this evening. I swear I was completely powerless against his influence when you were not nearby! But as soon as you confronted Krampus tonight, his possession over me was defeated and I instantly realized how I must have hurt you! That's why I fell to the ground in despair! The realization and the guilt overwhelmed me once the spell was broken! Please forgive me, Santa, I beg of you. Only you can keep me safe from the demonic powers that want to hurt us both! Now that evil Krampus is banished from our home, we can go back to how it used to be!"

"I'm still waiting to hear the GOOD reasons for me not to destroy you!"

Mrs. Claus scooted herself out from under Santa and sat up on her knees in front of him. She looked up toward Santa and managed to grin, as she concluded, "Because I bake the best damned cookies and give the best damned head on the planet. That's why!"

Santa returned the grin, adding, "Well, my dick isn't going to suck itself."

Mrs. Claus reached up and unfastened Santa's belt. "This is the only Christmas present I want to unwrap!"

She undid his fly and grabbed his erect cock, which had gotten rock hard when he was slaughtering the reindeer girls. Krampus had trained her mouth well, so she had no reservations about accepting the prickly present past her lying lips. She sucked like her life depended upon it, which it did. Her tongue licked like its sole purpose was to give pleasure, which it now was. Her throat opened freely to accept his thrusts, and her stomach uninhibitedly accepted his seed.

When she finished licking his dick clean, she grabbed him around the hips and promised, "My body will always be available for you to use... or abuse."

"Yes," he agreed. "We may need to drop by the Counseling Room later."

"As you desire, Master."

CHAPTER 12

With Rudolpho, Krampus and the Succubi gone from the castle, Alfie was able to work unencumbered in the workshop. A steady beam of noontime daylight from an unblocked window enabled him to confidently construct a wooden cross, which could be held in one hand, and to sharpen two thick wooden stakes. Although it was midday and Christmas was over, he sang the familiar refrains of his favorite hymn, "Silent Night."

When he was finished, he rose from the workbench and gathered his new tools, along with a wooden mallet. He walked silently, but boldly, to the bedroom of Santa and Mrs. Claus. He soon realized that he had to set his tools down in order to open the door.

Alfie opened the bedroom door slowly, and as quietly as possible, but then had trouble picking up the scattered tools from around his feet. His tiny hands fumbled with the tools and some of them dropped to the floor, causing a racket. He cursed himself under his breath.

He tried again to pick up the cross, stakes and mallet, but clumsily dropped them again.

After several attempts, he managed to grab all the tools and to approach the sleeping caskets of Santa and Mrs. Claus. The rustic wooden caskets had strange markings on the sides, such as "SEMI-FRAGILE" and "THIS SIDE UP," because they had been made from the box that the kids came in. The caskets were also mounted on pedestals, which didn't impede Santa or Mrs. Claus from accessing the lids, but made them out of reach for a munchkin like Alfie.

Alfie looked around the room until he set his eyes on a chair near the wall. He carefully placed the tools on the ground and retrieved the chair, positioning it in front of one of the caskets. Of course, when he went to pick up his tools, they slipped from his sweaty hands and clamored at his feet. He cursed himself again, but more quietly this time. After several attempts, Alfie managed to grab hold of everything and climb onto the seat of the chair.

With his hands full, Alfie realized he had no way to open the coffin lid. He tried moving all the tools to his left hand and under his left arm, allowing his right hand and arm to be unencumbered. But when he tried to lift the lid with his right hand, he lost his balance and tumbled off the chair. From his crumpled position on the floor, Alfie looked up and saw a shadowy figure in the doorway.

The figure crept forward and Alfie recognized 202499, who had been abandoned and forgotten in the castle infirmary. The boy mumbled something, but it was incoherent because his mouth was still swollen and he had no teeth. 202499 helped Alfie get back on his feet.

Alfie whispered, "Can you pick up the tools while I climb back onto the chair?"

202499 mumbled in the affirmative, nodding to ensure his meaning was communicated.

Once Alfie was back on the chair and 202499 was holding all the needed instruments, Alfie tried with both hands to lift the lid off the first casket. But he still couldn't get the heavy lid to budge.

Showing his frustration, Alfie testily whispered down, "Hand me the mallet and one of the stakes."

202499 handed Alfie the mallet, and then began inspecting the two stakes.

Alfie, in a more impatient whisper, instructed, "Either one is fine, just give me a stake."

202499 gave Alfie one of the stakes and then offered the little man the cross too.

"Did I ask for the cross?" Alfie asked in a louder tone.

202499 mumbled in the negative, and shook his head to ensure his meaning was communicated.

"Then I must not need the cross yet," Alfie tensely explained.

202499 attempted to give Alfie a "thumbs up" signal, but ended up dropping the cross and the second stake. Alfie rolled his eyes while 202499 leaned down to pick up the items.

Alfie put the tip of his stake against the seam of the coffin lid and tapped it lightly with the mallet. Alfie froze in fear when a rumbling was heard inside the casket.

He waited a few moments and then tapped the stake again, this time with a little more force. Again the tapping caused a disturbance inside the box.

Alfie waited a bit longer, and then hauled off and smacked the stake hard with the mallet.

This time the wooden tomb exploded apart, sending into the air wooden planks, Alfie, his chair, his tools and his helper. Santa burst from the broken wood and landed on his feet on the floor, just as the casket of Mrs. Claus busted apart in the same manner.

The unconscious bodies of Alfie and 202499 were then grabbed by the merry makers and tossed around like rag dolls, their limp figures slamming violently against the walls and floor of the bedroom. Santa then bent over the body of Alfie, while Mrs. Claus leaned over 202499. When the vampires prepared to feed upon their prey, they suddenly halted and gazed upon each other with queer gaunt expressions on their hideous faces. They both tried again to feed, but their mouths only produced sloppy sucking and slurping sounds against the nubile necks of the victims.

Santa leaned back on his haunches and placed his fingers into his own yap and began desperately feeling around. Mrs. Claus performed the same mouth inspection and immediately began sobbing.

Santa raised his fists in the air and screamed toward the ceiling, "Krampus! What have you done?! Just wait 'til I find you!"

EPILOGUE

Somewhere in an Amazon kind of jungle or foresty place, Krampus turned to Rudolpho and said, "My ears are burning. And when I say that, I mean that my ears are burning more than a demon's ears would usually burn."

Two muscular male Incubi, holding machetes and wearing loin cloths like they were future Chippendale dancers, glanced at each other in confusion and shrugged their bare manly shoulders.

"Rudolpho," Krampus continued. "Which way do we go now?"

Rudolpho looked down at a compass and pointed with his free hand. "According to my calculations, we need to cut right through this foliage."

"You heard him boys!" commanded Krampus.

The Incubi began cutting a path through the thick overgrowth of vines and verdure. Krampus and Rudolpho followed, sporting the latest wide-brimmed explorer's hats.

Eventually, the party reached a vine-covered cottage, where Krampus tapped on the door with his riding crop. A glowingly gorgeous young redhead, wearing nothing but a green grass skirt and some strategically-placed fronds across her blossoming bosom, opened the cottage door. She seductively grinned at the tall sweaty Incubi, until Krampus cleared his throat and she looked down at the little devil.

Krampus asked, "I assume you are the Tooth Fairy?"

The Tooth Fairy smiled at Krampus and nodded.

"I've come with a business proposition for you," Krampus announced. "But first I'd like to present you with a little gift."

Krampus held out a jewelry box and opened it for her to see the contents. A splendidly sparkling, startlingly stunning, set of wondrous wings spontaneously sprouted from the shoulders of the titillated Tooth Fairy as soon as she set her glowing green eyes upon the two perfect pairs of bloody vampire fangs.

ABOUT THE AUTHOR

After an unillustrious print journalism career in southwestern Pennsylvania, Rich Bottles Jr. moved to West Virginia at the age of 32 to pursue a career in technical writing.

He spends his free time visiting and hiking at the many state parks in the Mountain State, which is also where he develops the concepts for his novels. He has produced a trilogy of WV-themed "humorrorotica" books, the most recent of which is *The Manacled*, set in the vicinity of the West Virginia Penitentiary. Other books in the series include *Lumberjacked* and *Hellhole West Virginia*.

Rich was a contributing editor on *The Big Book of Bizarro*, *Westward Hoes* and *Rise of the Dead* anthologies by Burning Bulb Publishing. He also helped create *The Tailsman* comic book with Gary Lee Vincent.

He has also written stories for the StrangeHouse Books anthologies *Strange Sex, Zombie! Zombie! Brain Bang!, Strange Versus Lovecraft, A Very StrangeHouse Christmas* and many others.

The Vampire Who Saved Christmas

MOTION PICTURE SCRIPT

By

Rich Bottles Jr.
with Gary Lee Vincent

© 2017 Burning Bulb Publishing
All Rights Reserved

THE OPENING SCENE IS A GAS-LIGHTED VILLAGE STREET DURING A
WINTER STORM WITH NO ONE IN SIGHT.

MOST OF THE VISIBLE STRUCTURES ARE DARK AND DREARY, BUT
THERE IS A SHOP AT THE END OF THE STREET THAT IS LIT WITH
NUMEROUS CANDLES THAT ARE TWINKLING AS IF THE STORE IS A
BEACON OF HOPE AND WARMTH.

CREDITS ROLL OVER THIS SCENE.

FOLLOWING THE CREDITS, THREE STRANGE FIGURES WALK PAST THE
STATIONARY CAMERA. ONLY THEIR BACKS ARE VISIBLE AS THEY
WALK TOWARD THE LIGHTED SHOP, BUT IT IS OBVIOUS THAT THE
CENTER FIGURE IS IN A HOODED ROBE (AKA REAPER-LIKE) AND HE
IS FLANKED BY TWO ALMOST NAKED WOMEN WHO ARE OBLIVIOUS TO
THE FRIGID ENVIRONMENT.

2   EXT/INT - SANTA'S TOY SHOP - NIGHT   2

The hooded character, KRAMPUS, is banging on the door of
the lighted shop with what appears to be some type of
riding crop. The door opens revealing ALFIE, a short
elf-type person, in a gayish outfit. Alfie's mouth pops
open in shock at seeing the weird trio.

                    ALFIE
          H-how may I help you?

                    KRAMPUS
          How about you scurry off and tell
          Jolly Ole Saint Nick that Krampus
          is here to see him on urgent
          business.

                    ALFIE
          Y-yes, sir, right away.

While they're waiting, the women take a couple of the
candles from the window and begin dropping hot wax on each
other in a sensually playful way.

Alfie returns to the front room.

                    ALFIE (cont'd)
          Mr. Claus will see you now.
          Please follow me.

The women are busy licking the wax from each other, but
Krampus smacks them with the crop and they all follow the
Elf to an office.

The office is gaudily decorated as would be expected.
Santa is standing behind a cluttered desk and there is one
guest chair in front of the desk. The trio passes Alfie,
who closes the office door and scurries away.

                    SANTA
          Ho, ho, ho! Or should I just say
          Hoe and Hoe? Anyway, come in!
          Come in and sit down! If it isn't
          my old nemesis, Krampus! Still
          thrashing and kidnapping bad
          kids, making my job a little
          easier? Ho, ho, ho!

Both Santa and Krampus sit down, while the women stand on
either side of Krampus, posing provocatively like they're
at a questionable photo shoot. Santa pushes forward a
plate of cookies on the desk.

                    SANTA (cont'd)
          Would any of you like a cookie?
          They're fresh-baked from Mrs.
          Claus.

                                        (CONTINUED)

The women leap forward to grab a cookie, but give no thanks and do not speak.

                    SANTA (CONT.)
          Ladies, I don't think we've been
          properly introduced. But I bet
          you were once on my naughty list.
          Ho, ho, ho!

                    KRAMPUS
          Here is Succubus Two and Succubus
          One. These things will bite you;
          they want to have fun.

                    SANTA
          Eh, what?

                    KRAMPUS
          Let's stop the small talk, Nicky.
          I've come here with a serious
          proposition for you.

                    SANTA
          Do you mind if I have a cookie
          while you tell me?

                    KRAMPUS
          Yeah, I do mind, fat ass. Maybe
          you eat too many cookies? Maybe
          Mrs. Claus is trying to kill you
          with all her sugary treats. Did
          you ever think of that, tubby?
          Well, have you?

                    SANTA
          Now, why would Mrs. Claus...

                    KRAMPUS
          You're getting old, Santa. You're
          way overweight. I don't even know
          how you lift your proverbial bag
          of toys. I made all my rounds
          last Christmas, but my
          confidential source tells me you
          barely made it back before dawn
          from your little benevolent
          giveaway campaign. Also, I heard
          certain presents didn't get to
          the intended recipients, causing
          grief and disappointment to
          interfere on an otherwise joyous
          Christmas morn?

                    SANTA
          Now, see hear, Krampus, I don't
          know where you're getting your
          information, but need I remind
                    (MORE)

                         SANTA (cont'd)
you that nobody's perfect?
Mistakes may be made, but you
have to look at the big picture -
the greater good...

                         KRAMPUS
Spoken like a true Communist,
Santa. You know as well as I do
that you cannot continue at the
pace you're currently on. You're
getting more and more feeble and
the greedy kids' wish lists are
getting longer and longer? And
you have "what" to help you? One
pint-sized fag, who doubles as a
toy-maker and a butler? God
forbid you ask Mrs. Claus to lend
a hand because she's too busy
baking up another batch of your
poison.

                         SANTA
So what exactly do you propose,
Krampus?

                         KRAMPUS
Not only can I help you live
forever, but I can provide an
endless supply of pint-sized
helpers.

                         SANTA
Really? You know Santa doesn't
like liars, Krampus.

                         KRAMPUS
I don't give a fuck what you
like, Santa, because I don't want
any of your junky gifts. But my
proposal will help both of us.
Succubus One and Succubus Two can
provide you a magic elixir that
will give you eternal life on
earth, Santa. Imagine living long
enough to see yourself
immortalized in poorly made
stop-action animation or being
used to promote Coca-cola...

                         SANTA
What are those things?

                         KRAMPUS
Accept the elixir and you'll find
out... in due time, of course.

                                        (CONTINUED)

                          SANTA
             But how does all this benefit
             you?

                          KRAMPUS
             I'm being overrun by the brats I
             kidnap every year. I barely have
             time to give each of them their
             daily thrashing. I weed out the
             older ones every year to try to
             make room for the new crop, but
             there's just too many bad kids
             popping up every Christmas.
             Personally, I blame the parents,
             but what can you do, right? The
             prospect of receiving coal from
             you never works and the threat of
             being beaten by birch rods and
             whips by me isn't working either.

                          SANTA
             Perhaps if they're socioeconomic
             situation improves, their
             behavior would also...

                          KRAMPUS
             Oh, shut the fuck up with that
             bleeding heart bullshit, Santa. I
             say we combine our operations. I
             say we set up a warehouse in some
             remote place, like the North
             Pole, and we put all my kidnapped
             brats to work making toys for
             your so-called "good kids." I'll
             be in charge of the manufacturing
             and you'll be in charge of the
             distribution. What do you say?

                          SANTA
             I say, bring on the succubi!

Krampus stands up to shake Santa's hand on the deal, while
the women cheer and clap their hands.

                          KRAMPUS
             Then I'll leave you and the girls
             alone, Santa, to work their
             magic!

After Krampus leaves the room, the girls and Santa begin
making out, eventually biting Santa's neck on both sides.
Ala 2 Girls 1 Cup, the women then take turns vomiting
blood in each other's throats, then eventually take turns
vomiting blood in Santa's mouth.

3   INT - KITCHEN - NIGHT   3

Krampus enters a kitchen area and smacks the plump bottom
of MRS. CLAUS with his crop. Mrs. Claus jumps, almost
dumping a steamy platter of cookies that she just removed
from the oven. She smiles at Krampus as she sets the pan
down on the table.

                    MRS. CLAUS
          Oh, Krampy, don't sneak up on me
          like that!

                    KRAMPUS
          You know I like the booty.

                    MRS. CLAUS
          So, did the old man fall for it?

                    KRAMPUS
          Like a pedophile priest to a
          choir, my dear.

Mrs. Claus starts taking off her apron while Krampus
starts unbuttoning her blouse.

                    MRS. CLAUS
          So, Santa told you about his days
          as choir conductor Priest
          Nicholas?

                    KRAMPUS
          Ha, ha! Good one my dear! Now
          bend over the table and press
          your tits into that hot cookie
          dough!

                    MRS. CLAUS
          Whatever you say, Master.

Krampus lifts up her skirt and begins plowing Mrs. Santa
from behind.

                    KRAMPUS
          Soon we'll be at the North Pole,
          or some OTHER remote place,
          together forever... While you
          keep filling Santa's mouth with
          cookies, I'll keep filling your
          holes with my Christmas cheer!

4   EXT - SANTA'S TOY SHOP - NIGHT   4

Outside Santa's shop - later that night. Krampus is by
himself, leaning against the building and smoking a pipe.
Suddenly the shop door bursts open from inside and a
menacing Santa appears).

                    SANTA
              Krampus! What have your witches
              done to me!

                    KRAMPUS
              What's up, Father Christmas?

Santa grabs Krampus by the collar and gets in his face,
Santa's new fangs glistening.

                    SANTA
              You said nothing about making me
              a vampire, you demon bastard!

                    KRAMPUS
                  (smiling)
              Did you prefer a werewolf?

Santa throws Krampus to the ground.

                    SANTA
              I'm not laughing, Krampus! You
              think this is funny?

                    KRAMPUS
                  (getting up from the ground)
              Chill out, Nicky. There's only a
              few paths to immortality, at
              least here on Earth. Vampirism
              seemed to suit you best...

                    SANTA
              How do you figure that?

                    KRAMPUS
              You work at night, right? Well,
              vampires can only go out at
              night, otherwise they'll shrivel
              up and die in the daylight.

                    SANTA
              Shrivel up and die?!

                    KRAMPUS
              Well, spontaneously combust,
              however you want to say it. But
              sorry, there'll be no more
              afternoon strolls in the park for
              you. Not that you did a lot of
              that...

                                        (CONTINUED)

                        SANTA
          What about Mrs. Claus? What is
          she gonna say when she finds out
          she's married to a vampire?

                        KRAMPUS
          Actually, she was next on the
          appointment list of Succubus One
          and Two.

                        SANTA
          What?!

Santa starts to run back into the shop, but Krampus grabs
him by the arm.

                        KRAMPUS
          Hold on there, Santa. Mrs. Claus
          knows all about what's going
          down. And she knows all the
          benefits of being a vampire.

                        SANTA
               (turns back around to face
                Krampus)
          Benefits of being a vampire?

                        KRAMPUS
          Yes, there are benefits. Benefits
          of being a vampire at Christmas.
          Follow me and I'll explain...

As they leave the storefront, the face of a very
frightened elf can be seen peering out from inside.

5   EXT - VILLAGE STREET - NIGHT   5

Scene changes to include both figures walking side by side
through the desolate, dark and snowy village streets.

                  KRAMPUS
             (walking along side Santa in
             the village)
As I was saying, there are
benefits...

                  SANTA
Benefits?

                  KRAMPUS
Yes, there are benefits...
             (breaking into song, circling
             Santa, dancing on the street)

There are benefits to being a vampire at Christmas

Benefits to the drinking of blood

For blood is the true color of Christmas

As white snow and green wreathes turn to mud

For the vampire, he stalks and seduces

He creeps through the ice and the snow

He grabs any neck that he chooses

Without the need to find mistletoe

If a vamp gains weight with his feasting

He need not worry of his obese condition

For he knows that his life's everlasting

And no mirrors will bear his reflection

When the elves have finished toy-making

They'll start work on a very large coffin

They'll decorate it with popcorn and string

So that Santa can sleep in Christmas morn

There are benefits to being a vampire at Christmas

Benefits to the drinking of blood

For blood is the true color of Christmas

And it'll run red through the streets like a flood!

6   EXT/INT - BORDELLO - NIGHT   6

Krampus and Santa stop outside a very large house.

                    KRAMPUS
          ... And we're here!

                    SANTA
          Here? This is a whorehouse.

                    KRAMPUS
          Indeed it is Santa. Indeed it is.
          Have you visited before?

                    SANTA
          I don't usually deliver gifts to
          whorehouses, Krampus.

                    KRAMPUS
          Really? Well, what if the whores
          have children living with them?
          Are you going to avoid those
          whorehouses?

                    SANTA
          Yes, because those children would
          be the sons and daughters of
          whores, would they not?

                    KRAMPUS
          I guess you got me there, you
          judgmental prick... Anyway, this
          particular place is not your
          everyday ordinary run-of-the-mill
          disease-ridden whorehouse. Oh,
          no, no, no! This particular house
          of ill repute is owned by my good
          friend Rudolfo and every whore
          inside was personally selected
          and supplied by me from my hoard
          of victims when they were still
          in their preteens. Rudolpho is
          going to assist us in our
          corporate merger and relocation
          plans.

Krampus knocks on the door with his crop and a large man
dressed as a modern/70's era stereotypical pimp opens the
door. He's wearing a large gold chain with a
diamond-studded "R" as the pendant.

                    RUDOLPHO
          Gentlemen! I've been expecting
          you. Please come in.

The three men enter a stereotypical velvety bordello
reception room. Rudolpho motions for the other two to be
seated.

                                        (CONTINUED)

RUDOLPHO (cont'd)
Can I offer either of you a
drink?

KRAMPUS
Schnapps, for me, thank you.

SANTA
I'll have egg nog if you've got
it.

RUDOLPHO
But of course.
    (Rudolpho leaves the room.)

SANTA
You still haven't told me why
we're patronizing a whorehouse.

KRAMPUS
Well, this is where you'll be
able to pick up a quick meal -
fast food, so to say. Also, as I
said, Rudolpho has offered to
help us in our joint venture.

SANTA
What's his incentive to help?

KRAMPUS
Not being attacked by you or Mrs.
Claus. You see, Rudolpho values
his earthly existence.

Rudolpho comes back into the room and hands out drinks.

KRAMPUS (cont'd)
Thank you, Rudolpho. Now let's
show Santa what's on the menu.

Rudolpho picks up a small bell from a table and rings it.
A parade of sparsely dressed women enter the room.

RUDOLPHO
(lyrically)
You know, Dasher and Dancer and
Prancer and Vixen. Comet and
Cupid and Donna and Blitzkrieg.

The women line up in front of the men. Maybe DASHER is
jittery, DANCER is dancing, PRANCER is prancing, etc. As
their names are called, each turns around to display their
names tattooed as tramp stamps above their asses.

SANTA
Blitzkrieg?

(CONTINUED)

                         RUDOLPHO
              She's sort of our Goth girl. But
              who cares if a whore is happy as
              long as she does her job, right?

                         KRAMPUS
                    (waving his crop)
              I'll thrash the attitude right
              out of her! Father Christmas
              needs happy concubines! Isn't
              that right, Santa?

Santa stands up and approaches the short-cropped
back-haired Blitzkrieg.

                         SANTA
              Who's your daddy?

Santa grabs her by the hair and twists her head to reveal
her neck. He savagely bites into her throat, holding her
up as he feeds. The other women gasp, but cannot look
away.

                         KRAMPUS
              Hey you, Dancer, get over here on
              my lap, pronto!

Dancer runs over and starts to perform a lap dance on
Krampus.

After awhile, Krampus looks over at Santa.

                         KRAMPUS (cont'd)
              Don't drain her out, Santa, you
              gluttonous pig! We need her for
              later!

Santa lets Blitzkrieg drop to the ground.

                         RUDOLPHO
              The rest of you ladies, help
              Blitzkrieg back to the dressing
              room and prepare your costumes!

Santa is wiping the excess blood off his mouth with his
coat sleeve as he approaches Krampus's chair. The girls
are in the background dragging Blitzkrieg away.

SANTA: So if I had drained the bitch, would she have
become a vampire?

Dancer is still grinding on Krampus's crotch, but Santa
ignores her presence. Dancer has a distressed look on her
face.

                                        (CONTINUED)

                    KRAMPUS
          No, she just would have died is
          all. You'd have to vomit the
          girl's blood back into her throat
          to convert her.

Dancer starts acting like she wants to throw up.

                    KRAMPUS (cont'd)
          What's wrong, Dancer, you don't
          like what you're hearing? Do we
          disgust your delicate whorehouse
          disposition? Maybe Santa has
          something to plug your mouth
          with, so you don't throw up over
          Rudolpho's fine carpetry.

                    SANTA
               (unfastening his pants)
          Yes, even I was careful not to
          spill any blood on the carpet.

                    RUDOLPHO
          Indeed, Dancer, you'd best not
          regurgitate on this carpeting.
          Lord knows not even Comet could
          get such a stain out!

7   EXT - BORDELLO BACK PORCH - NIGHT   7

Santa, Krampus, and Rudolpho are walking out onto the back
porch of the bordello.

                    KRAMPUS
                (pointing)
            Check out what Rudolpho procured
            for you, using my specifications
            of course!

                    SANTA
                (walking forward into the
                snow-covered backyard with a
                surprised look on his face)
            This is awesome! You've really
            outdone yourselves, Krampus and
            Rudolpho!

CAMERA PULLS BACK TO VIEW THE TRIO APPROACHING A HUGE RED
SLEIGH. HARNESS LINES ARE SPREAD OUT IN THE SNOW IN FRONT
OF THE SLEIGH.

                    SANTA (cont'd)
            But what will we use to pull such
            a massive sleigh?

Rudolpho pulls the bell out of his coat pocket and rings
it. In pairs, the women trot out of the back door and line
up in front of the sleigh. The women are dressed as "pony
girls," with leather straps across their bodies, clip-on
antlers atop their heads and long-haired tails sprouting
from their asses.

The men work on securing the women to the harnesses, who
are silent except for some horse noises. Krampus has to
smack a few of them with his crop to keep them in line.

                    KRAMPUS
            Go, ahead and jump inside, Santa.
            Take her for a spin around the
            village and see how she handles.

                    SANTA
                (climbing aboard and
                grabbing a long horse whip
                from inside)
            Don't mind if I do, Krampus.
            Don't mind if I do!

Santa cracks the whip against the bare back of the closest
pony girl. She lets out a squeal and pushes against the
girl in front of her. The sleigh begins to jolt forward as
Santa cracks his whip against the next closest girl.

                                            (CONTINUED)

                              SANTA (cont'd)
                    Now, Dasher! Now, Dancer! Now,
                    Prancer, and Vixen! On, Comet!
                    On, Cupid! On, Donna and
                    Blitzkrieg!

As the sleigh pulls out of the scene, Rudolpho breaks out
in song.

**HO HO (RUDOLFO'S SONG): Sang to a similar melody/beat as
WAY DOWN by Elvis Presley**

LINE 1:

I know it's hard to fathom

But try to stay right here.

We've lots of pretty women

To serve as your reindeer!

Right at your disposal

A sleigh of sluts so fast

To take you "round the world"

From each mouth hole to their ass!

Can you see it...(see)

See it...(see)

See it...(see)

See it?! (see!)

CHORUS:

Ho Ho

Take your sleigh and try out the snow

Ho Ho

Grab your sluts and away you go

Ho Ho

There may be things that you don't know

Ho Ho

Don't worry...just go!

(with your ho's)

8   EXT - SANTA'S TOY SHOP - NIGHT   8

Santa's sleigh pulls up on the street outside his
workshop. Mrs. Claus comes out of the shop to greet him

                    MRS CLAUS
              That's quite an impressive rig
              you've got there, Santa!

                    SANTA
              (jumping off the sleigh)
              Indeed it is, wifey, and all
              courtesy of Krampus and Rudolpho!

                    MRS. CLAUS
              (baring fangs)
              I wouldn't mind sinking my new
              fangs into that pimp Rudolpho.

                    SANTA
              Sorry to disappoint you,
              sweetheart, but Rudolpho is
              strictly off the menu for us.
              It's part of the agreement
              Krampus made with Rudolpho for
              his assistance. But you're
              welcome to dine upon any of these
              fine reindeer here, although you
              may want to steer clear of
              Blitzkrieg, since she's been
              pretty-well drained by yours
              truly.

                    MRS. CLAUS
              Which one is Blitzkrieg?

                    SANTA
              They all have their names
              tattooed on their asses.

                    MRS. CLAUS
              Fair enough. I'll even provide my
              lucky reindeer with some cookies
              after I feed, which should
              restore her energy following the
              involuntary donation.

                    SANTA
              You might want to give Blitzkreig
              a couple cookies too since she's
              still acting a bit sluggish.

                    MRS. CLAUS
              Oh, by the way, please drop
              inside the shop for a while and
              see, Alfie. He's been wanting to
              speak to you privately.

                                        (CONTINUED)

                    SANTA
          All right... That little piece of
          shit never could accept change.

9   INT - SANTA'S TOY SHOP - NIGHT   9

Scene moves inside to Santa's office. The elf-like ALFIE
is sitting on the guest chair, while Santa is seated
behind the desk. Santa can barely see the top of Alfie's
head over the edge of the desk)

                          SANTA
               You wanted to talk to me, Alfie?

                          ALFIE
               Yes, Santa, there seems to be a
               lot of changes taking place
               around the shop and I'm concerned
               about what my future role will
               be?

                          SANTA
               What changes are those?

                          ALFIE
               Excuse me?

                          SANTA
               The changes you've observed. What
               are you talking about?

                          ALFIE
               Well, for instance, you and Mrs.
               Claus becoming blood-thirsty
               vampires, for one...

                          SANTA
               Oh, yes, that. I see.

                          ALFIE
               And you conspiring with Krampus,
               a known child-molesting demon
               from the depths of hell.

                          SANTA
               Changes, indeed, my friend. You
               are quite observant, I must say.

                          ALFIE
               Uh, thank you, I guess.

                          SANTA
               So you're worried that these
               minuscule changes to our business
               plan may adversely affect your
               current state of employ?

                          ALFIE
               Sorta, yes.

                                        (CONTINUED)

                    SANTA
          Alfie, how much are we paying you
          now for your butler and
          toy-making service?

                    ALFIE
          Nothing.

                    SANTA
          Nothing, eh? As in zero?

                    ALFIE
          Correct, sir. I get paid zero
          salary for my services.

                    SANTA
          But we do provide you with room
          and board.

                    ALFIE
          Yes, if you consider room and
          board to be sleeping in a closet
          and eating stale cookies.

                    SANTA
          And now you're worried about
          losing all these benefits?

                    ALFIE
          Well, I am a Christian and it
          looks like I may be the only
          truely good person currently
          involved in this devilish
          enterprise.

                    SANTA
          Well, it's always good to have a
          decent person around to bounce
          ideas off of and keep us focused
          on our ultimate mission of
          altruistic philanthropy.

                    ALFIE
          I'm glad to hear that is still
          our mission, sir.

                    SANTA
          Of course it is, Alfie. Just
          because I'm now a so-called
          blood-thirsty vampire and I'm
          teaming up with a demon from
          hell, doesn't mean I don't want
          to provide all the good children
          with presents on Christmas Eve!

(CONTINUED)

                         ALFIE
             Okay...

                         SANTA
             Also, when we set up our new
             shop, some of your toy-making
             burden will be relieved and I'll
             make sure you get an actual room
             to live in, so your queer self
             can finally come out of the
             closet.

                         ALFIE
             My queer self, sir?

                         SANTA
             Is there anything else, Alfie?

                         ALFIE
             Well, there is, but I'm hesitant
             to say anything...

                         SANTA
                  (baring his fangs)
             Out with it, fag! I don't have
             all day!

                         ALFIE
                  (visibly shaken and
                  trembling)
             I - I - I don't trust this
             Krampus character, Santa. I think
             he has a less than honorable
             interest in Mrs. Claus.

                         SANTA
             Do you have any evidence of this
             serious accusation toward my new
             business partner?

                         ALFIE
             N - No, sir, I just have my
             suspicions.

                         SANTA
             Well, until you have proof, I'd
             advise you to keep your
             dirty-minded suspicions to
             yourself.

                         ALFIE
             Yes, sir.

                                                     CUT TO:

A scene of Mrs. Clause feeding on a reindeer.

10   EXT - APPROACHING CASTLE - NIGHT   10

CAPTION ON SCREEN: Some indeterminable time later...

A VAST WASTELAND OF SNOW IS SEEN AT NIGHT - THE SNOW
REFLECTING THE MOONLIGHT. NOTHING INDICATES THAT THIS IS
THE NORTH POLE OR ANYWHERE ELSE SPECIFIC. TRAMPING IS
HEARD IN THE SNOW AND THEN SUCCUBUS ONE AND SUCCUBUS TWO
ARE SEEN CARRYING THE FRONT AND BACK END OF A LITTER-TYPE
CARRIAGE, WHICH WE ASSUME CONTAINS KRAMPUS.

A marching song, without instrumentation, is then heard
from a chorus of female voices, occasionally accompanied
by a whip crack. As Santa's sleigh comes into view, with
Santa, Mrs. Claus and Alfie inside the sleigh, the voices
are revealed to be coming from the reindeer.

Santa's sleigh and Krampus's litter both have torches to
light the way.

REINDEER SONG

Marching, marching,

Driving through the snow,

Our hot bodies are freezing,

From our toesies to our nose.

Marching, marching,

Hiking 'cross this ice,

Our battered legs are tiring,

While the whip takes a slice.

Marching, marching,

How long can we go on?

We're weak from their feeding,

And our souls now are gone.

Marching, marching,

Oh look how we suffer,

Our hope it is fleeting

As our trek gets tougher.

Marching, marching,

Like the soldiers of Bataan

(CONTINUED)

Or the men who are missing

From the jungles in Vietnam.

Marching, marching,

We're hungry and we're cold,

Our guts are all cramping,

From the plugs we must hold.

etc.

Finally, Alfie, with opera glasses held to his face,
speaks up and points ahead.

>   ALFIE
>   De Place! De Place, boss! De
>   Place!

>   SANTA
>   (snatching the glasses from
>   Alfie)

>   GIMME THOSE!

A large castle-like structure can now be seen in the dark
distance.

>   SANTA
>   (cracking his whip)
>   He's right! Krampus's place can
>   be seen up ahead! Now, Dasher!
>   Now, Dancer! Now, Prancer, and
>   Vixen! On, Comet! On, Cupid! On,
>   Donna and Blitzkreig!

A TIME FADE EVENTUALLY PUTS THE SLEIGH IN FRONT OF SOME
STABLES. SANTA GRABS A SHOVEL BESIDE THE STABLE WALL AND
HANDS IT TO ALFIE. HE ALSO REMOVES A TORCH FROM THE SLEIGH
AND HANDS IT TO ALFIE.

>   SANTA (cont'd)
>   Alfie, see to it that the
>   reindeer are locked into their
>   stables and given some unfrozen
>   water. Also, once you remove
>   their tails, you may need this
>   shovel to clean up.

>   ALFIE
>   Yes, sir!

>   SANTA
>   Come, Mrs. Claus, and let's
>   inspect the facilities. Perhaps
>   (MORE)

                          SANTA (cont'd)
          we can find some food for the
          reindeer. We want to keep them
          healthy and strong, after all.

11   INT - CHRISTMASLAND - NIGHT   11

Santa, Mrs. Claus, Krampus and the Succubi approach the
entryway. The huge doors suddenly burst open and Rudolpho
is revealed in the threshold.

                    RUDOLPHO
            Ladies and gentlemen, welcome to
            Christmasland! The place where
            every good boy and girl wishes
            they could visit and hang out
            with Jolly Ole St. Nick and his
            horny concubines!

As the group walks past Rudolpho, he speaks to Mrs. Claus

                    RUDOLPHO (CONT.)
            No offense meant toward you, of
            course, Mrs. Claus.

                    MRS. CLAUS
            None taken, Rudolpho.

Rudolpho closes the massive doors.

                    KRAMPUS
                (looking around at the large
                 entry room, with its wall
                 torches and large fireplace)
            I love what you've done with the
            place, Rudolpho!

                    RUDOLPHO
                (grabbing a torch)
            Thank you, Krampus. Let's do a
            quick tour of the facility, shall
            we? Follow me... We'll start with
            the bedrooms down this hall.

Rudolpho opens the first door they come to and walks
inside a spacious bedroom, which includes a large bed, a
fireplace, and various other furnishings.

                    RUDOLPHO (cont'd)
            This is the master bedroom,
            reserved for Mr. and Mrs. Claus,
            of course. It features the
            largest bed that I could locate
            in the fall catalog, considering
            Santa's massive accouterments.

                    SANTA
            Excuse me?

                    RUDOLPHO
                (ignoring)
            Also, please notice the absence
            of windows, which means none of
                    (MORE)

                                        (CONTINUED)

                    RUDOLPHO (cont'd)
          that nasty sunshine can penetrate
          the room.

                    MRS. CLAUS
                    (glancing quickly toward
                    Krampus without Santa
                    seeing)
          Hopefully, there'll be some
          penetration in here.

                    SANTA
          Excuse me?

                    RUDOLPHO
                    (ignoring)
          Notice this empty side of the
          room, which is eventually where
          your new sleeping coffins will be
          placed. In the meantime, you'll
          have to sleep on the bed like us
          normal folk.

                    SANTA
          Excuse me?

                    MRS. CLAUS
          When will our sleeping coffins be
          ready, Rudolpho?

                    RUDOLPHO
          The construction will commence as
          soon as the first shipment of
          Krampus kids arrives, which
          should be in a day or so,
          according to the traffickers.

                    KRAMPUS
          Yes, before the first brat even
          thinks about making a toy, I'll
          make sure they finish your
          permanent sleeping quarters.

                    SANTA
          And make sure they use quality
          wood. I don't want to rest in
          some stinky pine box like a
          filthy peasant.

                    KRAMPUS
          But of course, Santa, I guarantee
          it will not be long before both
          you and Mrs. Clause can finally
          Rest in Peace, so to say.

                                        (CONTINUED)

                    RUDOLPHO
               (walking toward the door)
          Very well then, let's continue
          our tour.

Santa is first out the door, following Rudolpho, while
Krampus allows the Succubi to go in front of himself and
Mrs. Claus.

                    KRAMPUS
               (leaning down to whisper in
               the ear of Mrs. Claus)
          Speaking of R.I.P., I plan to rip
          these clothes off you later on.

                    MRS. CLAUS
               (whispering back)
          Promises, promises, Krampus.
          You'll have to find a way to
          distract the fat man long enough
          to rip off anything.

                    KRAMPUS
               (smacking her butt lightly
               with his crop to get her
               moving toward the door)
          Not a problem, sweetheart. No
          problem at all.

All the characters are now back in the hallway. Rudolpho
leads them to the next door, opens it and walks into a
similarly-sized room containing three beds and various
pictures on the walls.

                    RUDOLPHO
          I've taken the liberty of
          designating this bedroom to
          Krampus, and to Succubus One and
          Succubus Two. Notice the three
          beds...

                    KRAMPUS
          Look girls, you don't have to
          sleep on the floor anymore.

The succubi jump up and down and clap wildly.

                    KRAMPUS (cont'd)
          Unless you disappoint me and I
          make you sleep on the floor.

The girls calm down.

                    RUDOLPHO
          Have you noticed the walls, my
          friend?

THE PICTURES ON THE WALLS ARE DRAWINGS OF DEPICTING SCENES

                                        (CONTINUED)

OF ANCIENT CHINESE GRAPHIC SEX LIKE ONE WOULD SEE IN AN
ILLUSTRATED VERSION OF THE KAMA SUTRA.

                    KRAMPUS
              (studying the pictures, with
              a hand under his chin, like
              some art critic)
          Ah yes, very nice. Very nice,
          indeed. Nothing like ancient porn
          to get the old juices flowing...
          Hey look, Mrs. Claus, this woman
          getting fucked in the ass looks
          like you!

                    SANTA
          Excuse me?

                    MRS. CLAUS
          Oh, Krampus, you are such a
          kidder. Isn't he funny, Santa?

                    SANTA
          Yeah, funny like a Shakespearean
          comedy, my dear.

After an uncomfortable silence, Rudolpho moves to the
door.

                    RUDOLPHO
          Let's continue on to my favorite
          room!

SANTA immediately follows as before, then the Succubi
follow, leaving Mrs. Claus and Krampus again at the end of
the line.

                    KRAMPUS
              (whispering)
          Shakespearean comedy? Of course,
          my favorite is the Taming of the
          Shrew. Don't you agree, my little
          shrew?

The group walks to the next door, which Rudolpho enters
first as usual.

THE ROOM IS FURNISHED EXACTLY LIKE HIS BORDELLO, IN FACT,
THE SAME SET CAN BE USED.

                    RUDOLPHO
          Welcome to my humble abode! As
          you can see, I brought the
          furnishings directly from
          Rudolpho's House of Whores. I
          shall be staying on here at
          Christmasland as the head chef,
          whoremonger and general middle
          management associate.

                                        (CONTINUED)

                    MRS. CLAUS
          As long as you let me make the
          cookies.

                    RUDOLPHO
          But of course, Mrs. Claus!

                    KRAMPUS
          Yes, you're a regular Renaissance
          Man, Rudolpho. Perhaps that's
          what the R represents on your
          gold chain.

                    RUDOLPHO
          Why thank you, Krampus, I try my
          best.

                    SANTA
          Will there also be a bedroom
          available for my half-man
          servent, Alfie?

                    RUDOLPHO
          Actually, I'm sorry that I didn't
          think of designating a special
          room for...

                    KRAMPUS
               (interrupting)
          ...for that little shit? Let him
          sleep in a closet for all I care!

                    MRS. CLAUS
               (surprised)
          Krampus!

                    SANTA
          Yes, I sort of promised the
          little fellow his own room here
          at Christmasland.

                    RUDOLPHO
          Might I make a suggestion?
          Perhaps he can have a cot in the
          toy-making bunker where the
          children will be sleeping when
          they're not working. I believe
          he'll be helping to manage that
          area anyway, am I right, Krampus?

                    KRAMPUS
          Humph, I suppose so.

                    RUDOLPHO
          Actually, I planned on taking our
          group to the toy factory next.

                                        (CONTINUED)

When the group turns around toward the door to exit, they
see Alfie standing in the doorway.

                    ALFIE
          My ears were burning.

                    KRAMPUS
               (slashing his crop)
          Clear the way or I'll make more
          than your ears burn, you
          quarter-liter queer!

The group, including Alfie, enter a large workshop/factory
area, which includes various hand tools and supplies, such
as wood and other building materials, along with work
benches, etc. There's also a collection of cots in one
corner and what appears to be a staircase leading down to
the basement in the corner.

                    SANTA
          Very nice, Rudolpho! I can see a
          great many toys being made in
          this workshop!

                    RUDOLPHO
          Thank you, I kind of bought out a
          hardware store and had it moved
          here.

                    KRAMPUS
          Yes and soon this room will be
          filled with the sights, smells
          and sounds of industry -- the
          hammering and sawing of
          woodworking and metalcraft, and
          the cries and moans of the busy
          workers!

                    MRS. CLAUS
          Rudolpho, where do those stairs
          lead in the back?

                    RUDOLPHO
          Ah yes, those stairs lead to a
          special counseling room where
          Krampus will escort any workers
          who might fall behind in their
          productivity.

                    ALFIE
          Like a dungeon?

                    KRAMPUS
               (pointing with his crop)
          I know, lil' man, why don't you
          scurry over to the sleeping area
          and pick out a cot for yourself
          before the workers arrive?

                                        (CONTINUED)

Alfie looks inquisitively toward Santa, who nods back in
response. Alfie then leaves the group to lay down on a
cot.

                    RUDOLPHO
               (clapping his hands)
          Let's proceed! We still have a
          couple special rooms to visit.
          Look! There's another special
          room right over here!

Rudolpho leads the group to a glass door inside the
workshop that has a sign on it, which reads SANTA'S
OFFICE. Rudolpho opens the door and allows the group to
look inside the smallish office space, which contains a
desk, a bookshelf, and other furnishings.

                    SANTA
          Ah ha! This is where I shall keep
          track of all the good children
          and read their Christmas
          correspondence!

                    KRAMPUS
          Yes, and don't forget to keep
          that Naughty List up to date too,
          so I know who to pick up on my
          rounds.

                    SANTA
          I haven't let you down yet, have
          I Krampus? You wouldn't know what
          to do if you didn't have access
          to my annual list of naughty
          children!

                    KRAMPUS
          Don't flatter yourself, fat
          man...

                    SANTA
          Excuse me?

                    RUDOLPHO
          Speaking of calories, we should
          all proceed to the room that Mrs.
          Claus has been waiting to see!
          Yes, the kitchen!

The group leaves Alfie behind in the workshop and exits
from the door where it entered.

                                             CUT TO:

FADE TO BLACK, UNTIL ANOTHER LARGE ROOM IS ILLUMINATED BY
RUDOLPHO'S TORCH. THIS ROOM IS AN INDUSTRIAL SIZED KITCHEN
WITH A COAL STOVE, VARIOUS POTS AND PANS, PUMP SINK,

                                        (CONTINUED)

SURFACE SPACE FOR FOOD PREPARATION, CABINETS, ETC. THE
GROUP ENTERS AND BEGINS LOOKING AROUND.

                    MRS. CLAUS
            Oh my, this is humungous!

                    KRAMPUS
            That's what she said.

Santa glares at Krampus, then walks toward a couple of
large bags piled on the floor. One bag is labeled as
CARROTS and the other is POTATOES.

                    SANTA
            Rudolpho, are these bags for my
            reindeer?

                    RUDOLPHO
            Yes, sir, they are!

                    SANTA
            You think of everything, don't
            you?

                    RUDOLPHO
            Like I've said, I always try my
            best. I want to make
            Christmasland the best place
            ever!

                    SANTA
                (picking up the large bags
                and throwing them across his
                shoulders like bags of toys)
            While you folks continue to
            explore the kitchen, I'm going to
            bring my reindeer some chow.

12 INT - CHRISTMASLAND SONG MONTAGE / RUDOLPHO'S ROOM - NIGHT 12

SCENE BEGINS INSIDE RUDOLPHO'S ROOM WHERE HE IS STANDING AT A WET BAR, MAKING HIMSELF A DRINK. HE IS HUMMING A CATCHY TUNE CALLED WELCOME TO CHRISTMASLAND.

He carries his drink to a large chair and sits, placing his drink on a side table. He picks up a bell and rings it, which produces two go-go girls in bikinis to the room. They stand in front of Rudolpho and begin dancing, also playing tambourines, as Rudolpho begins singing.

Welcome to Christmasland!

Welcome. Welcome!

Come enjoy the holiday!

Welcome. Welcome!

When you are in Christmasland

You'll always feel at home!

When you are in Christmasland

You'll never feel alone!

CUT TO:

ALFIE ALONE ON HIS COT, STARING SADLY AT THE CEILING.

Welcome to Christmasland!

Welcome. Welcome!

Come enjoy the holiday!

Welcome. Welcome!

When you are in Christmasland

You can pull up any seat!

When you are in Christmasland

There's always lots to eat!

CUT TO:

SANTA DUMPING VEGGIES INTO THE STABLE TROUGHS.

(Bridge):

Now if you are a German,

I will tell you Willkommen!

(CONTINUED)

And if you're from Honduras

I will say Bienvenidos!

But if you're from Saudi Arabia

You can go suck a pissy labia!

Welcome to Christmasland!

Welcome. Welcome!

Come enjoy the holiday!

Welcome. Welcome!

When you are in Christmasland

There's never any fears!

When you are in Christmasland

There's never any tears!

                                                    CUT TO:

DUNGEON WHERE KRAMPUS IS WHIPPING A TEARFUL
SPARSELY-DRESSED MRS. CLAUS.

Welcome to Christmasland!

Welcome. Welcome!

Come enjoy the holiday!

Welcome. Welcome!

If you stay in Christmasland

You'll see some lovely lasses!

For when you live in Christmasland

The love flows like molasses!

                                                    CUT TO:

SANTA FEEDING OFF A REINDEER'S BLOODY THROAT.

(Bridge):

Now if you are a Chinaman,

I will greet you with Foon-yen!

And if you're a South Korean

I will say Hwan-yan Ham-ee-doh!

                                                    (CONTINUED)

But if you're from that Northern Side

You can go tongue a whore's backside!

Welcome! Welcome! Welcome! Welcome!

Welcome to Christmasland!

                                                        CUT TO:

BACK TO THE DUNGEON WHERE KRAMPUS CONTINUES TO ABUSE MRS.
CLAUSE, WHO IS EITHER STRAPPED TO A WOODEN X STRUCTURE OR
HER ARMS ARE SUSPENDED ABOVE HER HEAD. THEN PAN OVER TO A
DARK STAIRWAY WHERE ALFIE IS HIDING AND TAKING NOTES ON
THE PROCEEDINGS.

13   EXT - TRAIN STATION - NIGHT   13

SCENE 13A -- 1ST ALTERNATIVE SCENE FOR WORKERS ARRIVE (IT MAY NOT BE FEASIBLE TO USE A TRAIN STATION WITH A STEAM ENGINE)

CAPTION ON SCREEN: A Day or So Later

THE HAND-CARRIED LITTER THAT KRAMPUS USED EARLIER IS CARRIED TOWARD A SMALL TRAIN STATION BY THE SUCCUBI. RUDOLPHO BURSTS THROUGH THE DOOR OF THE LITTER.

                    RUDOLPHO
                (to the camera)
          Who were you expecting?

Rudolpho walks up to the ticket window and looks at a large sign that reads "PolEx," sort of like FedEx.

                    RUDOLPHO (CONT.)
                (speaking to a clerk through
                the window)
          Ah yes, can you tell me if the
          Polar Express is running on time?

                    CLERK
          What are you talking about?

                    RUDOLPHO
                (pointing to the sign)
          I assume Pol Ex is short for
          Polar Express?

                    CLERK
          No, it's short for Poland
          Express, you Pollack.

A whistle is heard in the distance.

                    RUDOLPHO
          Never mind smart ass.

When the train arrives at the station, Rudolpho walks up to a box car and works to open the heavy metal door handle. When the door is suddenly slid open, a handful of raggedy children fall out onto the snow.

                    RUDOLPHO (CONT.)
          Welcome to Christmasland! Get up,
          get up, get up, you little
          urchins. Your free ride is over.
          You'll be hoofin' it the rest of
          the way!

Rudolpho walks back to the litter and drags out a bunch of wooden snowshoes.

                                        (CONTINUED)

                         RUDOLPHO (CONT.) (cont'd)
          I know you brats aren't used to
          receiving gifts, but my friend
          Alfie made these snowshoes for
          you. So strap them on your feet
          and follow my carriage.

****

SCENE 13B -- **2ND ALTERNATIVE SCENE FOR WORKERS ARRIVE
(MORE BUDGET FRIENDLY)**

CAPTION ON SCREEN: A Day or So Later

Rudolpho answers a knock at the front door. A man in a
delivery uniform is standing outside with a clipboard.
Instead of a patch on his shirt that states FedEx, his
patch reads as PolEx.

                         RUDOLPHO
          Ah ha, I see you're with the
          Polar Express.

                         DELIVERY PERSON
          What are talking about?

                         RUDOLPHO
               (pointing to the patch)
          I assume Pol Ex is short for
          Polar Express?

                         DELIVERY PERSON
          No, it's short for Poland
          Express, you Pollack... Please,
          just sign for the delivery so I
          can leave.

Rudolpho leans further out of the doorway and sees a large
wooden crate.

                         RUDOLPHO
          How in the hell did you get that
          here?

                         DELIVERY PERSON
          You don't want to know... Please,
          just sign for the delivery so I
          can leave.

                         RUDOLPHO
               (grabs the man's clipboard
               and signs the paper)
          All right, already. Here. It's
          signed. Are you happy now?

                                              (CONTINUED)

                    DELIVERY PERSON
                   (walking away)
              Thank you, sir. You have a nice
              day.

                    RUDOLPHO
              Fuck off.

Rudolpho leans inside and yells.

                    RUDOLPHO (CONT.)
                   (screaming)
              Alfie, get your ass out here and
              bring a crowbar if those things
              even exist!

Rudolpho walks up to the wooden crate. There's a red arrow
painted on the side, pointing downward, which reads "THIS
SIDE UP". More upsidedown writing states "SEMI-FRAGILE.
HANDLE WITH SOME CARE." There are also a few air holes
drilled into the side, which Rudolpho leans over to try to
look inside.

                    ALFIE
                   (creeps up behind Rudolpho)
              Hey!

A startled Rudolpho jumps up and glares at Alfie.

                    RUDOLPHO
              Don't be sneaking up on people
              like that!

                    ALFIE
              Sorry. I did find a pry bar.

                    RUDOLPHO
              Then why aren't you prying the
              fucking crate open?

                    ALFIE
              I'm getting right on that, sir.

Alfie works to pry open one side of the crate. Once he's
successful, a handful of raggedy children fall out onto
the snow.

                    RUDOLPHO
              Welcome to Christmasland! Get up,
              get up, get up, you little
              urchins. Your free ride is over!

                    ALFIE
                   (speaking to the children
                   like Schwarzenegger)
              Follow me if you want to live...
              I mean, follow me and I'll show
              you your new living quarters.

                                              (CONTINUED)

                        RUDOLPHO
                (as the children stumble
                past him and enter the
                castle behind Alfie)
        Seriously though, if any of you
        don't follow him, I'll personally
        strangle the life out of you.

14   INT - SANTA'S TOY SHOP - NIGHT   14

SCENE OPENS INSIDE THE WORKSHOP AS THE CHILD LABORERS ARE
SEATED AT WORK BENCHES AND ALFIE IS WALKING AROUND GIVING
INSTRUCTIONS.

                    ALFIE
          I see you've already been given
          registration numbers, which is
          good. Santa himself will address
          you all later. My name is Alfie,
          but you should refer to me as
          Sir. I am the shop foreman and
          I'll be supervising you in the
          making of toys that Santa will
          deliver to the good children on
          Christmas Eve.

Alfie walks over to Santa's office.

                    ALFIE (CONT.)
          Basically how this will work
          is... I will receive toy lists
          from Santa that the good children
          have sent him. I'll review these
          lists and make notes as to what
          patterns or plans to use in the
          construction of the toys. Then
          I'll assign the lists to you so
          you can begin work on the toys.
          It's important that you work on
          one list at a time, so that no
          child's gifts get mixed up and we
          can avoid any disappointments on
          Christmas morning.

Alfie walks over to some filing cabinets.

                    ALFIE (CONT.) (cont'd)
          This is where the plans for the
          toys are kept. If you have
          difficulty finding something or
          understanding a pattern, just let
          me know because I've built all
          these toys over and over again.

Alfie walks to a wall where some tools are displayed.

                    ALFIE (CONT.) (cont'd)
          You all have some basic tools at
          your workbench, but here are some
          others that may help you in the
          construction of certain toys. We
          also have plenty of paints, glues
          and other accessories. If you
          can't find something, don't
          hesitate to ask...

40.

15   INT - KITCHEN - NIGHT   15

MRS. CLAUS IS BAKING AND SANTA IS EATING COOKIES AT THE
TABLE.

Rudolfo enters the kitchen.

            RUDOLPHO
      Excuse me, but Alfie is finishing
      up his orientation and the
      workers are expecting to hear
      from you, Santa.

            SANTA
        (sighs and gets up from a
        chair)
      Very well then.

Once Santa leaves the kitchen, Rudolpho turns to Mrs.
Claus who is pulling a tray of cookies from the oven.

            RUDOLPHO
      And Krampus requires your
      presence in his bedroom, Mrs.
      Claus.

            MRS CLAUS
        (placing the tray on the
        counter to cool)
      Very, very well then!

                                  CUT TO:

16   INT - SANTA'S TOY SHOP - NIGHT   16

SANTA ENTERS THE TOY SHOP AS A CHILD IS ASKING ALFIE A
QUESTION.

> ALFIE
> Ah yes, those stairs lead to a
> special counseling room where our
> product inspector, Mr. Krampus,
> will escort any worker who might
> be lacking in their productivity
> or their attitude. Believe me,
> you want to avoid such counseling
> at all costs.

> SANTA
> (making his presence known)
> You got that right, Alfie!

> ALFIE
> Hello, Santa, the workers have
> been waiting to hear from you!

> SANTA
> Very well then, you're excused
> Alfie.

> ALFIE
> (walking toward the exit)
> Yes, sir.

As Alfie leaves the workshop, Santa moves to the front of
the workbench area in order to address the workers.

SANTA'S ADDRESSES THE WORKERS IN SONG.

Because you're young you may believe

That the very meaning of life

Is full of nothing but birds and bees

But there's also struggling and strife.

For I am here to tell you all

As your mentor and your friend

That some people's lives shall befall

To painful anguish that won't end.

Some people are born privileged

It's really not their choice

While others' lives are pillaged

(CONTINUED)

And they'll never have a voice.

Life's not fair; get used to it

Your needs aren't worth my spit

Life's not fair; get used to it

As your future turns to shit.

But even the doomed are useful

Yes even you workers can help

For you can serve the good people

As part of the proletariat.

So don't be jealous of others

Who have much more than you

Treat them like sisters and brothers

Who give you their chores to do.

Like Christmas is a time of giving

As Jesus's birth proclaimed

All your sins, he has forgiven

But your service is ordained.

Life's not fair; get used to it

Your needs aren't worth my spit

Life's not fair; get used to it

As your future turns to shit.

SHOTS OF THE SHOCKED CHILD LABORERS WITH MOUTHS AGAPE OR
TEARY EYES.

CAPTION (pops up on screen): Meanwhile...

                                                   CUT TO:

17   INT - KRAMPUS' BEDROOM - NIGHT   17

KRAMPUS, DRESSED IN A BATHROBE, IS IN HIS BEDROOM ON A
CHAIR, READING SOME NASTY BOOK AND MUNCHING ON SOMETHING
FROM A CUP. HE HEARS A KNOCK.

>   KRAMPUS
>   Come in, my dear!

Mrs. Claus enters and closes the door.

>   MRS. CLAUS
>   (walking toward Krampus)
>   What are you eating, my dear? Are
>   my cookies not good enough for
>   snacking?

>   KRAMPUS
>   (looks in the cup, then
>   holds it out for Mrs. Claus
>   to see)
>   I'm snacking on human teeth,
>   sweetie. Would you like some?

>   MRS. CLAUS
>   Eww!

>   KRAMPUS
>   Don't knock it, hun. The
>   consumption of human teeth by a
>   demon provides a sexual virility
>   that mere mortals can never
>   attain.

Krampus places his cup and book on a side table, and opens
his robe.

>   KRAMPUS (cont'd)
>   (grinning)
>   Check it out, Mrs. Claus!

>   MRS. CLAUS
>   (unbuttoning her top)
>   I've got something for you to
>   check out too.

>   KRAMPUS
>   (licking his lips as he
>   stands up)
>   Did I mention that eating human
>   teeth also makes my tongue more
>   versatile?

>   CUT TO:

18   INT - HALLWAY - NIGHT   18

ALFIE IS LEANING OVER AND PEERING INTO THE KEYHOLE OF
KRAMPUS'S ROOM. HE THEN LOOKS DOWN AT HIS CLIPBOARD AND
MAKES SOME NOTES ON WHAT HE IS WITNESSING.

                                                 CUT TO:

19   INT - KRAMPUS' BEDROOM - NIGHT   19

A "TONGUE CAM" IS USED, THE POV CAMERA SHOWING THE TOP OF
A LONG TONGUE AS IT EXPLORES THE SKIN OF MRS. CLAUS.

                    MRS CLAUS
          Lick it up, lick it up, ooh yeah,
          come on, come on... Lick it up,
          lick it up, ooh uh!

                    KRAMPUS
                 (slurping)
          Certainly, my dear. In fact, I
          foresee a rock star career in my
          distant future!

                    MRS. CLAUS
          Oh, shut up and give me a KISS!

MORE "TONGUE CAM" SHOTS FOLLOW.

20   INT - CHRISTMASLAND - NIGHT   20

CAPTION: Closer to Christmas Eve...

SCENE OPENS IN THE WORKSHOP WITH ALL THE CHILD LABORERS
BUSY MAKING TOYS AS THEY SORROWFULLY SING A CHRISTMAS
STANDARD, REPEATING THE LYRICS OVER AND OVER LIKE ZOMBIES.

A CAPELLA (public domain)

Toyland, toyland

Little girl and boy land

While you dwell within it

You are ever happy there

Childhood's joy land

Mystic merry toyland

Once you pass its borders

You can ne'er return again

CAMERA TRAVELS TO ONE WORKBENCH AFTER ANOTHER SHOWING SAD
CHILDREN BUILDING TOYS. AT THE LAST WORKBENCH, A SAD BOY
SINGS A DIFFERENT TUNE OVER TOP OF THE OTHERS' SONG WHILE
HE WORKS.

NOTE: THIS BRIEF SONG IS INTENDED TO BE A RUNNING GAG - AT
THE END OF THE STORY, ALFIE WILL SING THIS TUNE AS "IT'S
SO HARD TO BE A CHRISTIAN AT CHRISTMAS."

It's so hard to be a Jewboy at Christmas.

It's so hard to be a kike on Christmas Eve.

I used to watch my friends light their candles

High upon a glorious Christmas Tree.

But I could only light a stick on the Menorah

And learn the shamash was just like me.

It's so hard to be a Jewboy at Christmas.

It's so hard to be a kike on Christmas Eve.

It's sad to know my ancestors killed Jesus

Though his teachings I refuse to believe.

All I ever got for my faith was a dreidel

So that's why I'm feeling so suicidal...

(CONTINUED)

(A loud clearing of a throat is heard off camera and the
boy turns his head to see Krampus standing beside him)

                    KRAMPUS
          Hey, 202499, let's take a walk to
          the Counseling Room.

                    202499
          I'm sorry, Mr. Krampus, I'll sing
          the song that I'm supposed to
          sing... Toyland, toyland...

                    KRAMPUS
          It's a little late for that now,
          202499. Let's go!

                    202499
                (slowly getting up, but then
                suddenly showing Krampus his
                project)
          But do you like my toy, Mr.
          Krampus?

                    KRAMPUS
                (while walking away with the
                boy, tugging his arm)
          To be honest, that wagon you're
          painting looks like crap.

                                        CUT TO:

21   INT - DUNGEON/COUNSELING ROOM - NIGHT   21

                    KRAMPUS
            (pointing to a seat that
            looks like a modern day
            dentist's chair)
        Take a seat over there, 202499.

Once the boy sits down, the Succubi come out of the
shadows and strap him into the chair, then disappear
again. The boy is obviously in distress.

                  KRAMPUS(CONT.)
            (parodying Herbie the elf
            from the Rudolf cartoon)
        I'm just not happy in my work, I
        guess. Some day I'd like to be a
        dentist. We need one up here.
        It's fascinating. You have no
        idea... Molars, bicuspids and
        incisors...

Succubi reappear, carrying trays of implements/tools,
including a set of pliers.

Krampus approaches the chair.

                  KRAMPUS(CONT.) (cont'd)
            (now parodying the Nazi from
            Marathon Man)
        Is it safe?

                  202499
            (stammering)
        Are-are, you talking to me, sir?
        Is what safe?

                  KRAMPUS
        Is it safe?

                  202499
        I-I-I can't tell you if something
        is safe, sir, if I don't know
        what you're talking about.

                  KRAMPUS
        Is it safe?

                  202499
        T-tell me what it is first.

                  KRAMPUS
            (evil laugh)
        Is it safe... to pull out all
        your fucking teeth!

(CONTINUED)

Succubus One pinches the boy's nose closed while Succubus
Two takes hold of his jaw. Krampus takes the pliers and a
rusty awl off the tray.

Krampus moves in toward the boy's mouth... scene
eventually fades out to the sound of screaming)

22   INT - SANTA'S OFFICE - NIGHT   22

SANTA LETTERS

CAPTION: Even closer to Christmas Eve...

SCENE INSIDE SANTA'S OFFICE. SANTA IS SEATED BEHIND HIS
DESK WHEN HE HEARS A KNOCK.

                    SANTA
                (dramatically)
            Enn-ter!

Rudolpho enters with a large bag and closes the door.

                    RUDOLPHO
            Mail call!

                    SANTA
            Just throw it down anywhere.

                    RUDOLPHO
                (fake pouting)
            But I thought I'd help you go
            through it today... Pretty please
            Mister Santa Claus... you
            promised you'd let me help...

                    SANTA
            All right, then. Sit the fuck
            down.

                    RUDOLPHO
                (sitting in the chair beside
                the desk)
            Thank you, thank you, thank
            you...

                    SANTA
            Give it a break Rudolpho. Now dig
            out a letter...

Rudolpho grabs an envelope out of the bag with his left
hand and snaps open a switchblade knife with his right
hand. He then cuts open the envelope with the blade and
pulls out the letter.

                    RUDOLPHO
                (clearing his throat)
            Ah-hem, Dear Santa...

Rudolpho stops to laugh and waves the letter toward Santa.

                    RUDOLPHO (cont'd)
            Ha! Oh look, the little retard
            spelled Dear as D - E - E - R!

                                        (CONTINUED)

                          SANTA
              Just read the damn thing,
              Rudolpho!

                          RUDOLPHO
              Okay, okay, already... Ah-hem,
              Dear Santa, my name is Mary and
              I've been very good all year.
              Please bring me a pony and the
              appropriate riding tackle. Some
              straw would also be nice. Thank
              you kindly, Mary.

                          SANTA
                   (reaching over the desk to
                   grab the letter)
              Give me that! She'll get a doll
              and like it.

As Santa writes notes on the letter, Rudolpho is busy
opening the next envelope.

                          RUDOLPHO
              This next one is from Billy..
              Ah-hem, Dear Santa, this has been
              a very hard winter for me and my
              family. My father has become ill
              and can no longer find work. My
              brothers and sisters don't want
              any toys for Christmas, but if
              you could bring us some food and
              maybe some medicine for father,
              it would be greatly appreciated.

Rudolpho lowers the letter and looks at Santa. Santa looks
back at Rudolpho. Both men's lower lips are trembling.
Then they both burst out in raucous laughter.

                          RUDOLPHO (cont'd)
                   (still laughing)
              Oh, oh, Santa, I don't want any
              toys for Christmas, but perhaps
              you could cook up a nice pot of
              stew...

                          SANTA
                   (laughing along)
              Oh, yes, and maybe bring some
              chicken soup for papa!

                                            CUT TO:

23   INT - KITCHEN - NIGHT   23

KRAMPUS AND MRS. CLAUS ARE IN THE KITCHEN.

                    KRAMPUS
          Cook me up some Chicken Soup for
          the Soulless, sweetheart.

                    MRS CLAUS
          But what if Santa interrupts?

                    KRAMPUS
          Don't worry, Rudolpho is keeping
          him busy in the office.

                    MRS CLAUS
             (jumping onto the table)
          In that case, let's get cookin'!

Krampus goes through the cupboards, pulling out various
ingredients, like sugar and flour and honey, etc., while
Mrs. Claus wriggles out of her clothes atop the table.
Krampus has trouble opening one of the lower cabinets and
eventually gives up on trying to open it. He then busies
himself making a mess out of Mrs. Claus. At one point, he
places some small bloody teeth onto her sticky body and
eats them off.

AT THE END OF THE SCENE, THE CAMERA FOCUSES ON THE
CUPBOARD THAT KRAMPUS HAD TROUBLE OPENING. IT IS NOW AJAR
AND ALFIE CAN BE SEEN PEERING OUT OF IT.

24   INT - SANTA'S OFFICE - NIGHT   24

CAPTION: Okay, it's Christmas Eve.

SCENE OPENS AGAIN IN SANTA'S OFFICE, WITH HIM SITTING
BEHIND HIS DESK AND HEARING A KNOCK.

                    SANTA
                (dramatically)
          Enn-ter!

Alfie sheepishly comes in with his clipboard and closes
the door.

                    ALFIE
                (reading from the clipboard)
          I've completed the pre-trip
          preparation review and all seems
          in order for tonight. Your
          so-called list has been checked
          twice. The designated presents
          are wrapped and loaded on the
          sleigh, except for some last
          minute requests that are still
          being worked by the toymakers.
          The reindeer have been fed,
          beaten and their tails embedded.

                    SANTA
                (perturbed)
          Fine. If there's nothing else,
          you can leave... I'm a busy man.
          It's Christmas Eve, you know.

Santa looks down at some paperwork on his desk. Alfie
hesitates about leaving, as though he wants to say
something.

                    SANTA (CONT.)
                (looks back up)
          I said, if there's nothing else,
          then ski-daddle!

                    ALFIE
                (stuttering)
          W-well, Santa, actually there is
          something else, though I'm, ahh,
          hesitant to...

                    SANTA
          Out with it, elf!

                    ALFIE
          Okay, okay. You remember back at
          the old shop when I expressed
          concern over the trustworthiness
          of your business associate Mr.
          Krampus?

                                        (CONTINUED)

                         SANTA
                    (drawing out the word)
               Yes?

                         ALFIE
               And you said not to bother you
               with my suspicions unless I had
               proof?

                         SANTA
                    (drawing out the word again)
               Yes?

                         ALFIE
               Well, I believe I've got proof.

                         SANTA
               Proof of what, Alfie?

                         ALFIE
               Proof that Mr. Krampus has been
               having an affair with... with...
               with Mrs. Claus.

                         SANTA
                    (laughing)
               Are you joking, Alfie? I
               sincerely doubt Mrs. Claus would
               let that demon dick bone her.

Alfie approaches Santa with the clipboard and holds it out
for him to view.

                         ALFIE
               Here are my notes of what I've
               witnessed...

Alfie begins flipping through page after page of stickman
figure type drawings, vaguely illustrating some kind of
undefined activity between the stick figures.

Santa has a perplexed look on his face, like he can't
believe that he's being shown a bunch of idiotic and
indistinguishable child-like drawings.

                         SANTA
               What the fuck are you showing me?

                         ALFIE
               Well, these are my notes of the
               liaisons I've witnessed between
               Mr. Krampus and Mrs. Claus.

                         SANTA
               So, you expect me to believe they
               let you watch them fuck and take
               notes?

                                                   (CONTINUED)

                         ALFIE
            No, no, no. I hid and watched.
            They had no idea I was around.

                         SANTA
            Listen, Alfie. You may be a good
            Elf on the Shelf kind of spy, but
            you suck at drawing. I have no
            idea what these pictures are
            supposed to be. At first, I
            thought you were wanting me to
            play Hangman or something.

                         ALFIE
            Oh...

                         SANTA
            But I have an idea. Why don't you
            just tell me what you saw?

                         ALFIE
                    (looking around the small
                    office)
            Oh-kay, I'll try...

Alfie puts down his clipboard and moves around some
furniture to make a wider space on the floor

NOTE: THIS SCENE DEMANDS A LOT OF COMIC TIMING AND
PHYSICAL PANTOMIME COMEDY. THE FOLLOWING DIALOG CAN BE
USED AS A FOUNDATION FOR IMPROVISATION.

SOME QUICK CUT-AWAY SHOTS OF A SHOCKED AND SLACK-JAWED
SANTA SHOULD ALSO BE EDITED INTO THE SCENE.

                         ALFIE (cont'd)
                    (jumps into the empty space)
            Okay, okay, okay, so I sneak down
            the dungeon steps
                    (creeping movements)
            and low and behold
                    (surprised look)
            there's Mrs. Claus tied
            face-first to this like large
            wood cross
                    (spreading his arms and legs
                    like he's crucified)
            she's wiggling around like she's
            trying to break free
                    (grinding... you get the
                    idea on the accompanying
                    movements)

                         ALFIE (CONT.)
            But like she's not really
            seriously trying to break free,
            because her wrists are tied to
                    (MORE)

                                           (CONTINUED)

                         ALFIE (CONT.) (cont'd)
          the top part and her ankles are
          tied to the bottom part, well,
          okay, it's more like a big wooden
          X than a cross, so her legs are
          spread, but she still has her
          underpants on like white lacey
          briefs and a top, but Krampus is
          standing right behind her with a
          whip and he starts slashing at
          her back and her ass, and she
          starts screaming like she's
          panicking, trying to get her
          wrists free, but she can't of
          course, and Krampus just keeps
          whipping away and her underwear
          starts ripping and falling apart
          and her flesh starts getting
          these red slash marks that are
          turning black and blue, but
          Krampus doesn't let up and Mrs
          Claus just keeps squalling,
          although soon its just sounds
          like crying and then sort of like
          a low whimpering, then Krampus
          suddenly stops and checks on her,
          I guess to see if she's fainted
          or something, but I guess she's
          awake 'cause I hear her whisper
          [in a female voice], 'More - I
          need more, Please whip me like
          the whore that I am,' and Krampus
          is like

                         ALFIE
                (with a heavy male voice)
          Say no more, I'm happy to oblige

                         ALFIE (CONT.)
                (with his normal voice)
          and would you believe, he starts
          whipping her again, but not for
          too long, 'cause I think she
          really does faint after awhile,
          which is when Krampus drops his
          whip and his pants and jumps in
          behind Mrs Claus, whose body is
          hanging limply from the cross or
          X or whatever you call it, he
          directs his giant cock straight
          up Mrs. Claus's asshole, I swear,
          no lube or nothing at all, and I
          kind of hear her groan like
          involuntarily, which gets louder
          and louder and louder as Krampus
          keeps pounding and pounding and
          pounding away at that tight ass,
                         (MORE)

                    ALFIE (CONT.) (cont'd)
until Krampus is the one groaning
as he shoots his load right up
her poop chute, but he doesn't
stop there, oh no, he's still not
satisfied with his disgusting
conquest, 'cause he cuts her down
from the cross and starts
slapping her face while she's on
the floor, until she sort of
regains like semi-consciousness,
at least enough for Krampus to
force her to lick his filthy cock
clean, and she laps it up like
she's having a dream about
visiting an ice cream store or
something... Then there's another
time where both of them are in
Krampus's room, and I'm like
outside looking through the
keyhole, and I see Krampus
teasing Mrs. Claus with his big
nasty beet red tongue, well he's
sticking it in her mouth, in her
ears, in her nose, in her cunt,
in her ass, in her arm pits,
licking everything from her eye
balls to her taint, leaving no
crevice untouched, while Mrs.
Claus is squirming and panting,
begging for more licks and pokes,
as his tongue literally wraps
around each tit while the tip
tweeks her nipples like a baby
calf suckling the mama milk cow,
then I see them collapse on the
floor in a heap and Krampus gets
on top of her and they kiss like
only the French can kiss, but he
doesn't stop there, 'cause I
could see his tongue just wrap
around hers and start tugging it,
like he's trying to tear her
mouth organ right out of her
flushed face, while at the same
time, he's driving his hard cock
into her wet fuckhole, her body
is like convulsing, but you could
tell she's loving every second of
it, until finally she comes, but
still can't say anything 'cause
Krampus has her tongue tied up
with hers, so she can only spit
and drool in response to the huge
orgasm she's having, which causes
Krampus to come, pulling out of
her slit just in time to spray
                    (MORE)

> ALFIE (CONT.) (cont'd)
> his cum into her open mouth,
> which was kind of sick, 'cause
> his own tongue was sort of in the
> way... Then there was the time
> they were in the kitchen together
> and Mrs. Claus was on the table
> and Krampus was dumping sugar and
> honey all over her body like she
> was some kind of decadent cake or
> fancy pastry or something, and
> she's like, 'Pour some sugar on
> me,' and he's like, 'You know
> what they call this recipe where
> I come from?' She says, 'No, what
> do they call this type of recipe
> where you come from?' Well, he
> starts licking and slurping the
> sweaty sweets off her body until
> he reaches her snatch, then he
> looks up to her and answers, 'The
> Arsitocrats!'

> SANTA
> (jumping up)
> Shut up! Shut up, damn you! I get
> the point! You saw them fucking!
> Christ, I'll deal with this shit
> later!

Outside the office in the workshop, the workers can hear
Santa screaming and cursing, and they all look very
frightened. They are then startled in their seats when
Santa bursts through his office door.

> SANTA (CONT.)
> (loudy singing over the
> childrens' frightened cries)

ANOTHER CHRISTMAS SONG

Christ, not another

goddamned Christmas!

There's never enough

time to prepare!

Please not another

goddamned Christmas!

It always brings

nothing but despair!

(CONTINUED)

CUT TO:

RUDOLPHO WHIPPING A HOE WITH A HANGER IN HIS BEDROOM.

>   RUDOLPHO
>   (loudly singing over a
>   woman's scream)

Christ, not another

goddamned Christmas!

Trying to keep the

ornery youngins in line.

Please not another

goddamned Christmas!

There's ne'er enough

Cheese for their whine!

CUT TO:

KRAMPUS IN HIS ROOM, SANDWICHED IN BED WITH THE SUCCUBI.

>   KRAMPUS
>   (loudly singing over the
>   groaing of the Succubi)

Christ, not another

goddamned Christmas!

Tis not this demon's

fav'rite time o' year.

Please not another

goddamned Christmas!

With humans play acting

like they've got good cheer!

CUT TO:

SANTA'S ROOM WHERE MRS. CLAUS IS DECORATING THEIR SLEEPING
COFFINS WITH GARLAND, ETC.

Note: if the crate scene was used earlier to deliver the
kids to the castle, then the coffins should look they they
were constructed using wood from the crate - i.e., some of
the words from the crate can be seen on the coffins.

(CONTINUED)

                         MRS CLAUS
                      (quietly singing)

Christ, I recognize your

birth on Christmas!

It's the most blessed

time of the year.

Please allow us to

celebrate Christmas!

Even though it's now

Satan we hold dear!

                                                         CUT TO:

SANTA'S OFFICE. IT IS DARK BUT HAS A SPOTLIGHT EFFECT OF
SOME SORT SHOWING ALFIE STANDING ALONE. HE HOLDS HIS
CLIPBOARD TO HIS CHEST AND SOLEMNLY/SINCERELY SINGS *SILENT
NIGHT* 'A CAPPELLA' BY HIMSELF, LIKE HE'S ON THE STAGE OF A
SCHOOL CHRISTMAS PLAY.

                                               FADE TO BLACK

25   INT - VICTORIAN HOUSE - NIGHT   25

SCENE STILL BLACK, THEN FADE INTO A MOONLIT EXTERIOR SHOT
OF A VICTORIAN STYLE HOUSE WITH TWO FLOORS. CANDLELIGHT
CAN BE SEEN IN THE WINDOWS. SLOWLY ZOOM IN TOWARD A FIRST
FLOOR WINDOW.

Note: The following scenes loosely follow the story line
of the poem "Twas the Night Before Christmas".

SCENE/CAMERA TRAVELS THROUGH THE WINDOW AND INTO A
CANDLELIT LIVING ROOM. ALL IS QUIET. CAMERA TRAVELS TO
SHOW A DEAD MOUSE IN A TRAP [NOT A CREATURE WAS STIRRING,
GET IT?]; AND THEN SHOWS STOCKINGS HUNG BY THE CHIMNEY.
CAMERA TRAVELS UP THE STAIRS AND INTO ONE BEDROOM TO SHOW
CHILDREN ASLEEP IN THEIR BEDS; AND THEN TO ANOTHER BEDROOM
TO SHOW A WOMEN [IN A KERCHIEF] AND A MAN [IN A CAP] IN
BED.

Sleigh bells suddenly break the silence and the man
springs out of bed, runs to a window, tears open the
shutters and throws up the sash [raises the window].

The man looks out the window, then rubs his eyes in
disbelief. From his POV, looking downward upon a snowy
lawn, Santa is seen in his sleigh, along with his reindeer
pony girls. The man faints on the floor.

A BLURRY SEQUENCE THEN COMES INTO FOCUS INSIDE THE
BEDROOM, TO INDICATE THAT THE MAN HAS REGAINED
CONSCIOUSNESS, JUST IN TIME TO SEE SANTA STANDING BESIDE
THE BED.

                    NARRATOR
          And then, in a twinkling, I heard
          in the room,the slurping and
          gnashing of a man in costume.

          As I shook my head and was coming
          around, down on my wife St.
          Nicholas came with a bound.

Santa jumps onto the man's wife on the bed.

                    NARRATOR (CONT.)
          The neck of my wife he held tight
          in his teeth and the mouth
          encircled her throat like a
          wreath.

          He had a scary face and a big
          round stomach, that shook when he
          fed, like some beast in a panic.

          He was vile and vicious, a right
          evil old elf, and I gasped when I
          saw him, in spite of myself.

                                        (CONTINUED)

                        A glare from his eye and a twist
                        of his head, soon gave me to know
                        I soon could be dead.

Santa glares at the husband on the floor, hisses at him,
then continues feeding.

                        NARRATOR (CONT.) (cont'd)
                        He whispered some words as he
                        continued his work. He fed more
                        from my wife, then turned with a
                        jerk.

                        And pointing his finger toward my
                        sniveling nose, he gave a quick
                        nod and out the door he did
                        close.

Santa whispers something to the wife and then points
menacingly at the husband on the floor, before leaving the
bedroom. After Santa leaves, the husband faints again.

Shortly after that, a whistle can be heard from outside,
then Santa's voice bellows off camera.

                        SANTA
                        Happy Christmas to all, and to
                        all a good night!

26   INT - CHRISTMAS HOMESTEAD #1 - BEDROOM - NIGHT   26

SANTA SCARES KIDS CHRISTMAS SCENE.

SCENE OPENS IN CANDLELIT BEDROOM - TWO CHILDREN ARE IN
SEPARATE BEDS.

>   SISTER
>   (whispering)
>   Are you awake, brother?

(Pause)

>   SISTER (CONT.)
>   (Whispering louder)
>   Brother, are you awake?

>   BROTHER
>   I am now. I was just dreaming of
>   sugar plums.

>   SISTER
>   Well, I fear that I cannot sleep
>   for it is Christmas Eve.

>   BROTHER
>   Which is all the more reason for
>   you to try to sleep, because
>   Santa may not visit if we are
>   awake.

>   SISTER
>   We've been good all year, so I
>   doubt Santa would skip our house
>   just because I have a dose of
>   sleeplessness.

>   BROTHER
>   Good night, sister.

(Pause)

>   SISTER
>   Brother, I have an idea.

(Pause)

>   SISTER (CONT.)
>   I say, brother, I have an idea.

>   BROTHER
>   What, sister? What idea do you
>   need to tell me about in the
>   middle of the night?

(CONTINUED)

                          SISTER
          I say we sneak down to the
          drawing room and we hide
          ourselves somewhere.

                          BROTHER
          Why ever would we want to do
          that?

                          SISTER
          So we can see Santa arrive, of
          course, you numb skull.

                          BROTHER
          Calling names will not help me
          agree with your silly idea.

                          SISTER
                (getting up and walking to
                the brother's bed)
          Oh, I'm so sorry, brother dear,
          please come downstairs with me. I
          promise we won't get caught.

                          BROTHER
                (sitting up in bed)
          How can you promise that?

                          SISTER
                (pulling on his arm)
          Because I just know we won't be
          caught, that's how.

                          BROTHER
                (getting out of bed)
          Okay, okay, but if I don't get a
          new spinning top, I shall be
          quite angry with you.

CHILDREN SNEAK FROM THE BEDROOM AND CREEP DOWN THE STAIRS
TO THE DRAWING ROOM.

THERE IS A LOVESEAT/SETTEE AGAINST ONE WALL AND A
FIREPLACE AGAINST ONE WALL. THE FIREPLACE HAS SOME
STOCKINGS HANGING ON IT.

                          SISTER
                (holding the brother's hand)
          Come, let us hide behind the
          settee!

As soon as they are hidden behind the loveseat, sleigh
bells can be heard from outside.

                          SISTER (cont'd)
          Oh, sleigh bells, brother. Do you
          hear them? Santa must be outside!

                                              (CONTINUED)

                        BROTHER
                    (whispering)
            Hush girl, or someone will hear
            us.

A tense silence then hangs over the scene until the loud
squeaking noise of a door handle is heard in another room.

                        SISTER
                    (whispering)
            I think Santa is trying to get in
            through the front door.

                        BROTHER
                    (whispering)
            Is it locked? Is he unable to get
            in?

                        SISTER
                    (whispering)
            Let us approach the hallway and
            we'll be able to see if the door
            is locked.

The two sneak out from behind the loveseat and creep
toward the entryway of the drawing room, so they can peer
down the hall toward the front door. The knob is twisting
violently and the door is shaking.

                        SISTER (cont'd)
                    (whispering)
            Look brother, the door appears to
            be locked.

                        BROTHER
                    (whispering)
            So, can Santa not enter?

Suddenly the twisting of the knob ceases and a loud
pounding sound erupts, like someone is trying to kick the
door in.

FROM THE KIDS' POV IT APPEARS THE DOOR IS ABOUT TO GIVE,
BUT THEN THE POUNDING STOPS.

                        BROTHER (cont'd)
                    (whispering)
            I think we need to go back to our
            hiding place.

The two children actually walk backward into the center of
the drawing room, in order to keep their eyes on the
entryway.

UNBEKNOWNST TO THEM AS THEY BACK UP, BEHIND THEM IN THE
FIREPLACE CAN BE SEEN TWO DANGLING BOOTS, WHICH SUDDENLY
DROP DOWN ONTO THE ASH-COVERED SURFACE.

                                              (CONTINUED)

Santa jumps from the fireplace and looks at the children,
who are just now turning around toward the rustling
sounds. Santa appears enraged and is still carrying the
bullwhip he uses on the reindeer.

                         SANTA
               What are you brats doing up at
               this hour?!

The children shriek and run back into the hallway.

                         SANTA (cont'd)
                       (pursuing)
               Get back here right now, you two!

Santa runs into a kitchen and begins tossing cooking
utensils around and tearing open cabinets.

                         SANTA (CONT.)
               Where are you? Come out before I
               really get mad!

Santa angrily leaves the kitchen and goes into another
room, which appears to be a bathroom. There is an old
style porcelain tub with a curtain surrounding it. The
curtain appears to move a bit and Santa slowly approaches
it.

                         SANTA (CONT.) (cont'd)
                       (lower but still menacing
                        voice)
               Ah ha! I know where you are, so
               you'd better come out...

Both frightened children burst from behind the bath
curtain and attempt to run past Santa. Santa misses his
grip on the girl, but grabs hold of the boy with his left
hand. He then uses his right hand to throw out his whip
toward the girl. The tail end of the whip wraps around
her.

                         SANTA
                       (picking up the boy to eye
                        level)
               Are you the good little boy who
               wanted the top?

                         BROTHER
                       (panicking)
               Y-yes, Santa.

                         SANTA
               Then watch this!

Santa jerks hard with his right hand, releasing the whip
and causing the girl to spin like a top.

                                              (CONTINUED)

                    BROTHER
          Sister!

Santa laughs hard while still holding onto the boy.
Eventually the girl collapses onto the floor.

                    SANTA
          Okay, boy, unless you want to see
          your sister really whipped, tell
          me where your mother is?

                    BROTHER
          M-my mother? W-why?

Santa throws the boy against the wall and stomps toward
the cowering kid.

                    SANTA
          Dammit boy, where is your
          mother's room?!

                    BROTHER
          She's upstairs, the second door
          on the left... Please don't hurt
          her...

                    SANTA
          I'm Santa Claus and I'll do as I
          please!

Santa stomps out of the bathroom, leaving the crying
children behind. He crosses the drawing room and heads up
the stairs.

He walks directly to the mother's room, opens the door and
enters, finding the bed empty.

Santa leans down and grabs the bottom of the bed with one
hand and flips it up, revealing a terrified woman
underneath.

He pounces on the woman and bites her.

In a short while, he whispers something in her ear.

He then turns his blood-covered face toward the open
bedroom door and sees the children.

                    SISTER
               (screams)
          Mama!

                    BROTHER
          Where's papa? What did you do
          with papa?

Santa laughs as he stands up.

                                        (CONTINUED)

                    SANTA
          I thought I told you two to get
          to bed!

The children run away crying.

                                             CUT TO

27   EXT - CHRISTMAS HOMESTEAD #1 - NIGHT   27

Exterior shot of the house's front door. A man is seen
pounding on the door with his fist.

                         PAPA
                      (yelling)
             Hey, someone let me in! I'm
             locked out of the house!

28   INT - CHRISTMAS HOMESTEAD #2 - BEDROOM - NIGHT   28

PRAYING MOTHER SCENE.

SCENE OPENS IN BEDROOM, LIT BY MOONLIGHT THROUGH A WINDOW.
TWO SINGLE-SIZED BEDS ARE IN THE ROOM, ONE CONTAINING A
SNORING FATHER AND ONE CONTAINING A PRAYING MOTHER.

                 MOTHER
            (hands clasped and praying
            aloud)
        And dear God, please keep our
        family safe from the evil that
        permeates this world. In Jesus's
        name I pray. Amen.

THE BEDROOM DOOR SLOWLY OPENS, BUT NO ONE CAN BE SEEN IN
THE ENTRYWAY.

The mother gets up, looks through the slightly open door,
but sees nothing.

               MOTHER (CONT.)
            (closing the door)
        That is strange, for I am certain
        I sufficiently closed that door.

The mother climbs back into her bed and clasps her hands
again.

              MOTHER (CONT.) (cont'd)
            (praying)
        Dear God, strange things happen
        frequently in this house and no
        explanation can be found. If evil
        lurks in our humble home, please
        protect us from whatever haunts
        these premises. In Jesus's name I
        pray. Amen.

IN A FEW MOMENTS, THE DOOR CREAKS OPEN AGAIN.

              MOTHER (CONT.) (cont'd)
        Oh my. Is someone there? Is that
        you children, still awake on
        Christmas Eve?

The mother looks over toward her husband, but is greeted
with louder snoring.

              MOTHER (CONT.) (cont'd)
            (getting up)
        That faulty door brings such a
        chill to this room. I must have
        my husband fix it tomorrow.

She shuts the door again, and wiggles the knob to ensure
it is securely closed.

                                      (CONTINUED)

As she begins to climb into the bed, she hears the door
open again.

She stands up, but is afraid to turn and face the doorway.

She can hear heavy breathing behind her.

                    MOTHER (CONT.) (cont'd)
                (mumbling)
            Oh dearest husband, why must you
            sleep so soundly when your wife
            needs you most?

                    SANTA
                (low and evil)
            I heard your prayers, mother.

                    MOTHER
                (gasps at the strange voice
                and drops to her knees
                against the bed, then prays
                at the bedside)
            Dear God, please, please, please
            protect me from...

                    SANTA
                (pulls her up by the hair)
            Don't you know who I am?

                    MOTHER
                (frightened)
            N-no. Are you here to hurt me?

                    SANTA
            Only if you scream.

                    MOTHER
            W-who are you?

                    SANTA
            Are you dense, woman? Look at my
            costume... This is Christmas Eve.

                    MOTHER
            Are you St. Nicholas?

                    SANTA
            Bingo.

                    MOTHER
            But why are you in my bedroom?

                    SANTA
            Because I need your help
            downstairs.

                                        (CONTINUED)

> MOTHER
> Must I? Can you not just leave me
> be?

> SANTA
> Do you want your children to get
> their gifts or not?

> MOTHER
> I suppose, but cannot my husband
> assist you downstairs?

> SANTA
> Be a good wife and let the man
> rest.

> MOTHER
> All right, I guess...

CUT TO:

29   INT - CHRISTMAS HOMESTEAD #2 - STAIRS - NIGHT   29

SANTA LEADING THE WOMAN DOWN THE STEPS. SANTA'S BAG OF
GIFTS IS VISIBLE ON THE FLOOR. NUMEROUS CROSSES AND
CRUCIFIXES ADORN THE WALLS.

                    MOTHER
               (reaching the landing)
          What can I help you with? Were
          you expecting cookies and milk? I
          fear we forgot to set them out
          this year.

                    SANTA
          Well, that would've been nice,
          but that's not why I brought you
          down here.

                    MOTHER
          Oh. Then what do you need.

                    SANTA
               (pointing toward the walls)
          I can't set out any presents in
          this room until you take down
          every single cross. Just the
          sight of them makes me queasy.

                    MOTHER
          Remove my Savior's crosses from
          the room? Are you not aware of
          the true reason we celebrate
          Christmas?

                    SANTA
               (sneering)
          Bitch, I don't give a shit why
          you celebrate Christmas, but if
          you want me to leave presents for
          your brats, you best get your ass
          moving on the re-design.

                    MOTHER
          But...

                    SANTA
          And if you continue to piss me
          off, I'll tear your fucking
          throat out!

The mother hurries to take the crosses down from the
walls, mumbling a prayer about walking through the valley
of death.

WHEN SHE IS FINISHED SHE HAS HER ARMS FULL OF THE CROSSES.

                                        (CONTINUED)

                    MOTHER
          Where should I put them?

                    SANTA
          You can shove them up your ass as
          far as I'm concerned! But get the
          damned things out of this room!

                    MOTHER
                    (distressed)
          Yes, sir.

The mother scampers toward a doorway leading to another
room and places the crosses on the floor, out of Santa's
sight.

                    SANTA
          Now come back here and get on
          your knees in front of me.

The woman obliges.

                    SANTA (CONT.)
          Start praying to me, like you
          were doing upstairs.

                    MOTHER
                    (crying)
          Pray to you?

                    SANTA
                    (reaching down to put the
                    woman's hands together)
          Yes, heathen. Clasp your hands
          together and pray to me as your
          Lord and Savior.

                    MOTHER
          But you're not my...

                    SANTA
          Did the God you were praying to
          protect you from me?

                    MOTHER
          W-what?

                    SANTA
          I said, the God you've been
          praying to for protection, did he
          protect you from me tonight?

                    MOTHER
          P-perhaps my faith isn't strong
          enough when...

                                        (CONTINUED)

                    SANTA
          Bullshit! If you want me to
          protect you from a certain death
          tonight, then you'd better start
          praying to me and you sure as
          hell better mean it!

                    MOTHER
               (bawling)
          Dear Santa, I pray for your
          protection. I do not wish to
          die...

                    SANTA
               (kneeling down beside the
               woman)
          Very good. Now show me your neck
          and I'll baptize you.

Santa bites into the mother's neck and finishes out the
scene with the usual whispering to her ear.

30   INT - CHRISTMAS HOMESTEAD #3 - NIGHT   30

HOT POKER SCENE.

SCENE OPENS SHOWING A POKER STOKING A FIRE INSIDE A
FIREPLACE, THEN ZOOMS OUT TO SHOW A WOMAN IN A ROBE
HOLDING THE POKER.

ONCE THE FIRE IS BLAZING, THE WOMAN PUTS THE POKER BACK ON
A RACK BESIDE THE FIREPLACE.

ZOOM FURTHER OUT TO SHOW A PARLOR ROOM WITH A LARGE CHAIR
IN THE CENTER AND A WOODEN STAND BESIDE THE CHAIR. THE
STAND HAS A LIT CANDLE AND BOOK ON IT.

THE WOMAN WALKS TO THE CHAIR, SITS DOWN AND BEGINS TO READ
THE BOOK.

A CLOCK OR SOME OTHER FILM DEVICE INDICATES THE PASSING OF
TIME. THE WOMAN IS SHOWN TO HAVE FALLEN ASLEEP IN THE
CHAIR WITH THE BOOK ON HER LAP.

(once again a clock shows the passage of more time)

                                                    CUT TO:

AN IDENTICAL SCENE AS THE OPENING SHOT, WITH A POKER
PRODDING AT THE LOGS IN THE FIREPLACE. BUT THIS TIME WHEN
THE CAMERA ZOOMS OUT, IT CAN BE SEEN THAT SANTA IS HOLDING
THE POKER.

HE PULLS THE POKER FROM THE FIRE AND ADMIRES THE RED HOT
TIP.

WHEN HE TURNS AROUND, THE CAMERA SHOWS THE WOMAN NOW TIED
TO THE CHAIR, HER MOUTH IS GAGGED AND THERE IS A TERRIFIED
LOOK IN HER EYES.

                         SANTA
                If there's one thing I truly hate
                about my job, it's when people
                leave a fire burning in their
                fireplace on Christmas Eve,
                especially when there's no other
                way to gain access to their
                fucking home! Seriously, bitch,
                do you want your kids to get
                gifts on Christmas morn?

He only gets muffled cries in response.

                         SANTA (cont'd)
                    (walking toward the woman
                    with the poker)
                But maybe you don't realize just
                how hot burning yule logs can be
                when you drop onto them through a
                         (MORE)

                                              (CONTINUED)

                              SANTA (cont'd)
                    chimney? Maybe I should show you
                    how hot your fireplace is...

Woman frantically shakes her head back and forth.

                              SANTA (CONT.)
                         (stops just in front of the
                         chair and makes a reference
                         to a famous line from
                         Reservoir Dogs)
                    Hey, are you familiar with the
                    Super Sounds of the Eighteen
                    Seventies?

Santa performs some back and forth strutting dance moves
in front of the chair as he hums the song "Stuck in the
Middle with You".

                              SANTA (CONT.) (cont'd)
                         (singing pleasantly with no
                         music)

Well, I don't know why I came here tonight

I got the feeling that something ain't right

I'm so scared in case you fall off your chair,

And I'm wondering how you'll get up those stairs.

Demons to the left of me, Elves to the right,

Here I am, sticking this poker on you.

Santa leans down toward the woman and opens the bottom of
her robe with his free hand, revealing her upper thighs.

Yes, I'm sticking this poker on you,

And I'm wondering what more I should do

It's so hard to keep this smile from my face,

Losing control, and I'm all over the place...

The woman is clearly in distress and tears are flooding
her face as Santa slowing moves the hot poker toward her
bare thigh.

The woman suddenly screams through her gag as dark
sizzling smoke rises past her panicked eyes.

Santa brings the smoking poker back up toward his face and
inspects the tip.

                                             (CONTINUED)

> SANTA (CONT.) (cont'd)
> I believe this needs a warm up.

Santa walks back to the fireplace as the woman sobs in
pain.

AS SANTA PRODS THE POKER BACK INTO THE FLAMES, A PUDDLE OF
URINE FORMS UNDER THE CHAIR.

> SANTA (CONT.) (cont'd)
> (walking back toward the
> chair)
> Don't worry, I didn't forget
> about the other leg. I'm all
> about equality for women, you
> know.

This time when Santa places the hot poker onto the woman's
thigh, her body convulses within her restraints until her
muffled screams fade away and she goes limp in the chair,
passed out from the pain.

Santa turns around and throws the poker into the fireplace
like a spear, then he leans back toward the woman and
bites her neck.

He feeds from the motionless woman for a moment, then
straightens up and begins slapping her face until she
regains some murmuring consciousness.

When he sees that she is somewhat awake, he leans back
down to whisper in her ear.

31   INT/EXT - SANTA'S TOY SHOP - NIGHT   31

SCENE OPENS IN THE DIMLY-LIT TOY WORKSHOP WHERE WORKERS
AND ALFIE ARE ASLEEP ON THEIR COTS.

SUDDENLY OFF-CAMERA SHRIEKS AND SCREAMS PIERCE THE
SILENCE. MANY OF THE WORKERS BEGIN CRYING IN FEAR, SOME
MUMBLING ABOUT WHAT IS HAPPENING, ETC.

                    WORKER CHILD
                (closest to Alfie's cot)
            What is that, sir? Who is
            screaming? Please wake up, sir!

                    ALFIE
                (waking and sitting up)
            What the hell is that?

Alfie jumps up, dressed in elf-like pajamas.

                    ALFIE (CONT.)
                (to the group)
            Hush now! I'm going to
            investigate! You all stay put and
            try to keep calm, for God's sake!

Alfie lights a torch at the fireplace and leaves the
workshop. The screaming continues.

As he hurries down the hall of bedrooms, the residents are
gathering in the hallway with their own torches...Krampus
and the Succubi, Rudolfo and a couple whores, and Mrs.
Claus.

                    MRS. CLAUS
            Does anyone know where that
            screaming is coming from?

                    RUDOLPHO
            It also sounds like it's coming
            from outside the castle!

                    KRAMPUS
            Follow me!

THE SCREAMS CEASE AS THE GROUP FOLLOWS KRAMPUS OUTSIDE.
THEY THEN HEAD TOWARD THE STABLE AREA.

                    MRS. CLAUS
                (looking in fear at
                something ahead)
            Oh my God! What has happened?!

                    RUDOLPHO
            Holy fucking shit!

                                        (CONTINUED)

                    KRAMPUS
          Dammit, what has that fat idiot
          done?!

CAMERA REVEALS A DREADFUL BLOODY PILE OF DEAD PONY GIRLS
STACKED UP IN THE SNOW, ALL QUIET NOW WITH THEIR THROATS
SLIT.

ALL CONTINUES TO BE QUIET AS THE CAMERA REMAINS FOCUSED ON
THE PILE OF DEAD BODIES.

SUDDENLY SANTA APPEARS TRIUMPHANTLY AT THE TOP OF THE
PILE. HE IS ENRAGED, HIS FANGS BARED AND HIS EYES RED AS
LASERS. SANTA POINTS TOWARD KRAMPUS AND MRS. CLAUS.

                    SANTA
          You two are fornicators!

ALFIE IS SEEN TREMBLING BEHIND RUDOLPHO, BUT SUDDENLY RUNS
BACK TOWARD THE CASTLE DOOR.

Santa jumps down off the pile of dead women and approaches
Krampus and Mrs. Claus. Mrs. Claus falls to her hands and
knees and begins bawling hysterically.

                    KRAMPUS
              (calmly)
          Santa, Santa, Santa, if you had
          read the fine print of our
          contract, you would've clearly
          realized that...

                    SANTA
              (in the face of Krampus)
          Shut the fuck up, Krampus! I
          don't give a shit what the
          contract says, our business
          relationship is over!

                    KRAMPUS
          Let's not be hasty, Santa, we can
          always get new reindeer. Isn't
          that right, Rudolpho?

                    RUDOLPHO
              (still shocked and scared)
          W-whatever Santa wants...

                    KRAMPUS
          There ya go, Saint Nick, whatever
          Santa wants, Santa will get. So
          let's you and I work this thing
          out.

                    SANTA
          There's nothing to work out! I'm
          hereby retired from this
          bullshit!

                                        (CONTINUED)

                    KRAMPUS
          But you can't retire...

                    SANTA
          When I had the childrens' mothers
          under my spell tonight, I
          commanded them to provide gifts
          to their kids on Christmas from
          this point forward.

                                        CUT TO:

32   EXT - STOP-MOTION ANIMATION SCENE - DAY   32

THE PREVIOUS DARK, DREADFUL SCENE SUDDENLY CUTS TO SOME
BRIGHT CHEERFUL STOP ACTION ANIMATION, FEATURING A BURL
IVES-LOOKING SNOWMAN AND A SMALL BOY IN AN OUTDOOR WINTRY
SETTING.

Reference: "Santa Claus is Coming to Town" classic anime

                    ANIMATED BOY
          Oh, so that's how the tradition
          began of parents buying the
          Christmas presents, but still
          telling their kids that Santa
          brought them?

                    ANIMATED SNOWMAN
          Yes, Billy, that's the night when
          Santa quit delivering presents
          and let the gift-giving part to
          the parents.

                                               CUT TO:

33   EXT - SANTA'S TOY SHOP - NIGHT   33

DARK SCENE OUTSIDE THE TOY SHOP / CASTLE.

                    KRAMPUS
          But how in the hell am I gonna
          know where the bad kids are if
          you don't keep track...

                    SANTA
          Krampus, are you not paying
          attention?! We're through! Take
          your Succubus One and Succubus
          Two and Suck Up Rudolpho and
          leave Christmasland, ASAP!

                    KRAMPUS
          Whatever, tubby, but I'll have
          you know I've been pursuing other
          business prospects outside of
          here and I planned on leaving
          anyway.

                    SANTA
          Good for you, motherfucker! Now
          get out of my sight and let me
          deal with my cheating wife!

                                        CUT TO:

34   INT - SANTA'S TOY SHOP - NIGHT   34

SCENE BEGINS INSIDE OF THE WORKSHOP WHERE ALFIE IS
ADDRESSING THE WORKERS.

                         ALFIE
              Listen up! Your work here is done
              and you need to leave
              Christmasland now! You're all in
              very grave danger! Santa has gone
              berserk and no one is safe!
              Follow me and I'll show you where
              the coats are that I made for
              each of you. You'll also have
              wooden snow shoes to help hasten
              your journey to wherever the hell
              you're going.

                                              CUT TO:

35   EXT - SANTA'S TOY SHOP - NIGHT   35

SANTA STANDS ABOVE THE CROUCHING AND TREMBLING MRS. CLAUS.
THEY ARE ALONE.

                     SANTA
          How could you do this to me with
          that demonic piece of shit?!

          Don't you know that I can SEE you
          when you[re sleeping?

          I KNOW when you're awake.

          I know if you've been bad or
          good, for Christ's sake!

                   MRS. CLAUS
                   (begging)
          Please forgive me, Santa!

                     SANTA
          Give me one good reason why I
          shouldn't tear you apart limb
          from limb!

                   MRS CLAUS
                   (singing)

There's a reason,

A reason for this season,

When families come together,

To forgive one another.

Yes, there's a reason,

Behind every rising sun,

The promise of a new day,

Where we put our hurt away.

That reason is our love,

Which flutters like a dove.

A gift for you and me,

From a power we can't see.

Yes, there's a reason,

Christmas is for everyone,

No matter your religion,

                            (CONTINUED)

Christmas spirit makes us one.

So there is a reason,

That no one's hopes undone

That no one's fears abide

From our kindness deep inside.

That reason is our love,

Which flutters like a dove.

A gift for you and me,

From a power we can't see.

> MRS. CLAUS (CONT.)
> (music continues but she
> speaks to Santa)
> Please Santa, Krampus put me
> under a spell and I had to do
> whatever he commanded. Just like
> you did with those mothers this
> evening. I was powerless against
> Krampus when you were not nearby.
> But as soon as you confronted
> Krampus tonight, his spell was
> broken and I realized how I hurt
> you. Please Santa, forgive me.
> Now that you banished Krampus, we
> can go back to how it used to be.
> Oh, please let me bake you some
> damn cookies!

> MRS. CLAUS (CONT.) (cont'd)
> (standing up and singing
> again)

Yes, there's a reason,

For us to stay and not run,

To jump o'er any hurdles

And work out all our troubles.

So there is good reason,

To believe this race is won,

To put the past behind us,

And rebuild our solemn trust!

Santa puts his arms around Mrs. Claus and they are
face-to-face as they begin to sing together.

(CONTINUED)

That reason is our love,
Which flutters like a dove.
A gift for you and me,
From a power we can't see...
They kiss.

                                        FADE.

36   INT - SANTA'S TOY SHOP - DAY   36

SCENE OPENS WITH ALFIE ALONE IN THE WORKSHOP. HE'S AT A
WORKSTATION THAT IS LIT BY SUNLIGHT SHINING THROUGH A
WINDOW.

THE CAMERA REVEALS HE HAS ALREADY CRAFTED A LARGE WOODEN
CROSS AND IS NOW SHARPENING ONE OF TWO WOODEN STAKES. AS
HE SHARPENS THE STAKE, HE BEGINS SINGING TO HIMSELF

               ALFIE
        (singing a different version
        of the earlier Jewboy song)

It's so hard to be a Christian at Christmas.

It's so hard to be a mick on Christmas Eve.

I used to watch my friends light their candles

High upon the glorious Christmas Tree.

But now I can only light a torch for lynching

The demons and vampires afore they get to me.

It's so hard to be a Christian at Christmas.

It's so hard to be a mick on Christmas Eve.

It hurts to know I still believe in Jesus

While living with heathens who don't believe.

All I get for my faith is to be called an oddball

So that's why I'm feeling so very suicidal...

Alfie then gathers up his cross, his two stakes and a
mallet and walks out of the workshop.

In the hallway with the bedrooms, Alfie slowly creeps up
to Santa's room.

HE SOON REALIZES HE HAS TO SET HIS TOOLS DOWN IN ORDER TO
OPEN THE DOOR. HE OPENS THE DOOR AS QUIETLY AS POSSIBLE
AND THEN TRIES TO PICK UP HIS TOOLS, BUT DROPS SOME OF
THEM, CAUSING A RACKET, AND HE CUSSES UNDER HIS BREATH.

He tries again to pick up the cross, stakes and mallet,
but again drops a couple of them. After several clumsy
attempts, he manages to grab everything and enter Santa's
bedroom.

Crossing the threshold, he looks back at the open door and
considers closing it, but then looks down at his full
hands and decides to leave the door ajar.

                                 (CONTINUED)

ALFIE CREEPS TOWARD THE CASKETS IN THE CENTER OF THE ROOM
AND QUICKLY SEES THAT THE LIDS ARE OUT OF HIS REACH,
BECAUSE THE CASKETS ARE ON PEDESTALS.

Alfie looks around the room and sees a chair, so he places
the tools on the floor and retrieves the chair. Once he
places the chair in front of the first casket, he tries to
pick up his tools, but drops some of them, causing a
racket, and he cusses under his breath. He tries again to
pick up the cross, stakes and mallet, but again drops a
couple of them. After several clumsy attempts, he manages
to grab everything and climb up onto the chair.

ALFIE THEN REALIZES HE HAS NO WAY OF OPENING THE CASKET
LID WITH HIS HANDS FULL. HE TRIES MOVING ALL THE TOOLS TO
HIS LEFT HAND & UNDER HIS LEFT ARM, MAKING HIS RIGHT HAND
FREE. BUT WHEN HE TRIES TO OPEN THE CASKET LID, HE LOSES
HIS BALANCE AND FALLS OFF THE CHAIR.

FROM HIS CRUMPLED POSITION ON THE FLOOR, ALFIE SEES A
FIGURE IN THE DOORWAY.

THE CAMERA REVEALS IT IS THE JEWISH BOY (I.E., 202499),
WHO OBVIOUSLY DID NOT LEAVE WITH THE OTHER WORKERS.

                    202499
               (mumbles incoherently -
               because he has no teeth)

                         ALFIE
               (getting up from the floor
               and approaching the boy)

                    WHAT?

                    202499
               (mumbles incoherently again;
               this time a caption is
               provided at the bottom of
               the screen which states:)
               I thought I'd stick around in
               case you needed my help.

                         ALFIE
                    (quietly)
               Help? I think I heard the word
               help somewhere in there. So, yes,
               since, you're here, I could use a
               hand.

The duo approaches the first casket. 202499 gathers the
tools from the floor while Alfie climbs back onto the
chair.

While 202499 stands by holding the tools, Alfie tries
opening the lid of the casket. But the lid won't budge and
Alfie becomes frustrated.

                                        (CONTINUED)

                          ALFIE (CONT.)
                        (whispering)
                Hand me the mallet and one of the
                stakes.

202499 hands the mallet up to Alfie, but then looks at
both stakes like he can't decide which one to give.

                          ALFIE (CONT.) (cont'd)
                        (angry whisper)
                Either one is fine. Just give me
                a stake.

202499 hands Alfie a stake.

                          202499
                        (then mumbles
                        incoherently while a screen
                        caption states)
                Do you need the cross too?

                          ALFIE
                        (angry whisper)

                WHAT?

                          202499
                        (again mumbles incoherently,
                        but a screen caption states)
                I asked if you needed the cross.

                          ALFIE
                        (angry whisper)
                Cross? I heard cross. Are you
                asking if I need the cross?

                          202499
                        (nods affirmatively)

                          ALFIE
                        (angry whisper)
                Did I ask for the cross?

                          202499
                        (shakes his head negatively)

                          ALFIE
                        (angry whisper)
                Then I must not need the cross
                yet.

202499 attempts to give a "thumbs up" signal, but drops
the cross and the remaining stake.

Alfie rolls his eyes while 202499 bends down to pick up
the tools.

                                            (CONTINUED)

Alfie then places the tip of the stake under the edge of the lid and taps it lightly with the mallet.

A BRIEF RUMBLING IS HEARD FROM INSIDE THE CASKET, WHICH CAUSES ALFIE TO FREEZE IN FEAR.

A few moments of quiet pass and Alfie taps the stake again, this time a bit harder.

AGAIN A BRIEF RUMBLING IS HEARD FROM INSIDE THE CASKET, WHICH CAUSES ALFIE TO FREEZE.

Alfie waits longer this time, but then smacks the mallet hard against the stake.

THIS TIME THE CASKET EXPLODES APART, TOSSING ALFIE AND 202499 TO THE GROUND.

SANTA BURSTS FROM THE BROKEN WOOD AND LANDS ON THE FLOOR, JUST AS THE CASKET CONTAINING MRS. CLAUS BURSTS APART.

202499 and Alfie appear unconscious on the floor as Santa and Mrs. Claus begin tossing them around like rag dolls, eventually throwing 202499 and Alfie against the wall.

Santa then bends over Alfie, snaps the elfin neck, and bites into Alfie's throat, while Mrs. Claus does the same to 202499.

As the vampires attempt to feed, they both suddenly have curious looks on their faces.

They continue their attempts to feed while the sounds of sloppy sucking and slurping are heard. Santa then raises his head and puts his fingers in his mouth.

His anger rises when he realizes his fangs are missing.

                    SANTA
              (enraged screaming to the
              ceiling)
          Krampus! What have you done?!
          Just wait 'til I find you!

37   EXT - RAINFOREST - DAY   37

THE SCENE OPENS IN A RAINFOREST. IT IS DAYTIME

                    KRAMPUS
          My ears are burning. And when I
          say that, I mean that my ears are
          burning more than a demon's ears
          would usually burn.

Two muscular incubus males, wearing loin cloths like they
are Chippendale strippers, look at each other in confusion
and shrug their shoulders. They are also holding machetes.

                    KRAMPUS(CONT.)
          Rudolpho, which way now?

                    RUDOLPHO
          (looking down at a compass
          and then pointing with his
          hand)
          According to my calculations, we
          need to cut right through there.

                    KRAMPUS
          You heard him boys, start
          cutting!

The incubi begin cutting a path through the heavy foliage,
and Krampus and Rudolpho follow.

Eventually the party reaches a vine-covered cottage and
Krampus knocks on the door with his riding crop.

The door opens to reveal a beautiful woman, who smiles
when she sees the men - especially the imcubi as they make
immediate eye contact. The woman and the incubi wink and
grin at one another in a flirtatious way.

                    KRAMPUS (cont'd)
          (clears his throat to get
          her attention)
          I assume you are the Tooth Fairy?

The tooth fairy smiles at Krampus and nods.

                    KRAMPUS(CONT.)

I have a business proposition for you, but first I'd like
to present you with a little gift.

Krampus hands her a jewelry box and she gladly accepts it.
When she opens the box, she can see two separate sets of
bloody vampire fangs. She grins widely, causing large
wings to sprout out behind her like a peacock.

                                END CREDITS.

(CONTINUED)

AFTER THE END CREDITS RUN, THERE MAY BE A CAPTION THAT
READS:

STAYED TUNED FOR "SANTA VS. THE TOOTH FAIRY."

End notes: While credits roll, it may be a good idea to
include a montage of pictures of Santa biting various
Victorian women in their beds, thus giving the impression
that Santa made numerous visits that night.

WEST VIRGINIA-THEMED HUMORROROTICA

BY RICH BOTTLES JR.

HELLHOLE WEST VIRGINIA

From the heights of Mothman's perch high atop the Silver Bridge in Point Pleasant to the depths of Hellhole Cavern in Pendleton County, evil lurks within the shadows as the sun sets upon the haunted hills and hollows of West Virginia.

Bizarro author Rich Bottles Jr. blows the coffin lid off horror genre clichés with this tour de force cast of Eco-friendly vampires, beach-yearning zombies and sex-starved she-devils.

LUMBERJACKED

If you are easily offended or do not possess a truly depraved sense of humor, this story may not be the light summer reading fare you desire. As for the four feisty female freshmen stranded on top of West Virginia's third highest mountain, they have no choice but to experience the sick, twisted debauchery and perverted mayhem described deep inside the tight unbroken bindings of this horrific missive.

Lumberjacked takes the reader to a nightmarish world where character development and aesthetic integrity are prematurely cut short by the swinging axes of maniacal lumberjacks, who are hell bent on death and destruction in the remote forests of Appalachia. And at the climax, when paranoia crosses over to the paranormal, Lumberjacked makes Deliverance look like a family raft trip down the Lower Gauley.

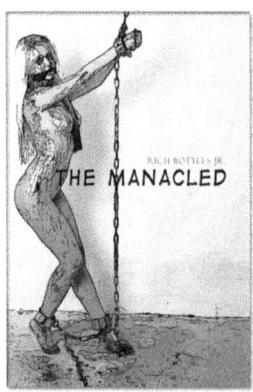

THE MANACLED

What happens when twin brothers lease out the former West Virginia State Penitentiary with the false purpose of filming a documentary on supernatural phenomena, but their true intention is to make a pornographic movie?

Chaos ensues as the disturbed spirits of murdered convicts, along with the reanimated dead from the neighboring Indian Burial Mound, take their vengeance on the unwary and undressed trespassers.

Zombies, ghosts, mobsters and porn collide in this bizarro tale from horror author Rich Bottles Jr.

Burning Bulb
PUBLISHING

WEST VIRGINIA-THEMED HUMORROROTICA

BY RICH BOTTLES JR.

BY

By

A collection of short stories from Rich Bottles Jr. Be forewarned that the graphic sex and violence described in this book of bizarre short stories may provoke psychological or emotional triggers for some unstable or weak-minded readers, including, but not limited to, the following extreme content: Rape, Torture, Murder, Mayhem, Kidnapping, Cannibalism, Necrophilia, Poisoning, Prostitution, Pornography, Nazis, War Crimes, Ethnic Cleansing, Terrorism, Incarceration, Bondage & Discipline, Sadomasochism, Corporal Punishment, Foot Fetishism, Masturbation, Alcoholism, Drug Abuse, Eating Disorders, Domestic Violence, Mental Illness, Suicide, Drowning, Religious Intolerance, The Occult, Adult Language, Homosexuality, Sodomy, Unwanted Pregnancy, Amputees, Adultery, Incest, Shoplifting, Bukkake, Penis Envy, Cigarette Smoking, and Heavy Metal Music.

THE VAMPIRE WHO SAVES CHRISTMAS

Cantankerous demon Krampus is out to ruin Christmas for everyone, but Mrs. Claus and Jolly Ole Saint Nicholas will do everything in their power to stop his diabolical plan, even if it means becoming vampires to fight the evil villain! Join Alfie the Elf, Rudolpho the Reindeer Trainer, and all the other merry residents of Christmasland in this hilarious yuletide adventure that is sure to become a joyous holiday classic!

THE TAILSMAN

He's hot on the trail, looking for some tail! Follow the adventures of Sly Franko in this ornery comic book set in the *Westward Hoes* universe by Gary Lee Vincent, Rich Bottles Jr., and Stuart Brown.

Burning Bulb
PUBLISHING

GARY LEE VINCENT'S
DARKENED
THE WEST VIRGINIA VAMPIRE SERIES

DARKENED HILLS

When evil descends on a small West Virginia town, who will survive?

Jonathan did not start out his life to become a rambler, it justworked out that way. William was a troubled youth with something to hide. Both were from Melas, a small town tucked away in the West Virginia hills... a town where disappearances are happening more and more frequently.

After the suicide of a wanted serial killer, the townsfolk thought the nightmare was over. But when a centuries-old vampire is discovered they find out the hard way it's just getting started. Dark secrets can only stay hidden for so long and when the devil comes to collect, there will be hell to pay. Can Jonathan and William find a way to stop the vampire before it's too late? Find out in *Darkened Hills!*

DARKENED HOLLOWS

In the heart-stopping sequel to the award-winning *Darkened Hills*, Jonathan and William must return to West Virginia to face possible criminal charges stemming from their last visit to the damned town of Melas, where both had narrowly escaped the clutches of a vampire seethe.

And as livestock start mysteriously getting murdered with all of their blood drained, worried farmers are searching for answers - leaving the local Sheriff and his deputy racing against time to learn the cause before a more violent crime is committed.

Burning Bulb
PUBLISHING

WWW.DARKENEDHILLS.COM

GARY LEE VINCENT'S
DARKENED
THE WEST VIRGINIA VAMPIRE SERIES

DARKENED WATERS

When the world goes to hell, the chosen must arise!

As Talman Cane orchestrates a flood of epic proportions in this third installment of the *Darkened* series the towns of Melas and Tarklin are caught completely off guard by the deluge. Hell-bent on finishing what they started, the evil brothers return to the lunatic asylum to take care of the witnesses and add to the ever-growing army of the undead.

Aided by Lucifer himself and the insane vampire demon Legion, the stage is set to channel all of the forces of hell to come forth. In an all-out race to survive, Jonathan, William, and Amanda soon discover they are up against impossible odds as Lucifer opens the Gateway to Hell, ushering in the zombie apocalypse and the End Times.

Find out who will survive this cosmic battle of the ages in *Darkened Waters!*

DARKENED SOULS

Melas and the Madison House are about to be rebuilt.
True evil is about to be reborne!

Young ex-priest and vampire-killer William is drawn back to the West Virginian town that almost killed him, where his vampire arch-enemy Victor Rothenstein still stalks the earth.

The town of Melas lies destroyed after the battle of the End of Days. But why is wealthy Jackie Nixon so eager to rebuild it using the bone dust of murdered souls?

Terrible evil has visited before, but the Gateway to Hell is about to be reopened in a horrific climax. And this time – it's personal.

www.DarkenedHills.com

Burning Bulb
PUBLISHING

GARY LEE VINCENT'S
DARKENED
THE WEST VIRGINIA VAMPIRE SERIES

DARKENED MINDS

Jackie Nixon intends to become Vampire Queen, but at what blood-drenched cost?

In this continuation to the explosive infernal saga begun in Darkened Souls, newly-turned vampire Jackie Nixon is taking no prisoners. Accompanied by her daughter, Kate, and by the captive vampire lord Victor Rothenstein, Jackie Nixon explores the Darkness. There, she intends to rouse the slumbering vampire race, bound under an ancient curse, and with their help, rule the human world.

But there's a deadly threat to Jackie's plans. Not just William who is trying to stop her, but her own royal ambitions. If Jackie performs the ritual to wake the sleeping vampires the wrong way, she could instead free the Red Beast of Hell, an unspeakable evil that even the undead fear.

DARKENED DESTINIES

With over 45 people missing after Jackie Nixon's party, the mysteries surrounding Melas and the Madison House keep getting darker.

Now, with legions of vampires at her command, can anything or anyone stop her from gaining complete control over all mankind?

The final battle has begun! As the Vampire Queen ascends her throne and sets to unleash the full forces of darkness, the fate of all things good hangs in the balance.

Burning Bulb
PUBLISHING

WWW.DARKENEDHILLS.COM

www.ingramcontent.com/pod-product-compliance
Lightning Source LLC
Chambersburg PA
CBHW061159170626
46809CB00003B/1167